The roll of thunder echoed across the rolling hills of western Kesh. Getting up in the late night Dunsor cursed as he walked to the single window in his small but modest home. He couldn't remember the last time it stormed this late in the season. It had to be at least ten or fifteen years to his inkling but then again he never understood why God sometimes did the things he did.

Dunsor walked slowly, his old limbs carrying the many years of toiling in the rich farming grounds of the village of West End. He ran a thick hand through his thinning gray hair as the rumble began to grow louder. By god the storm was moving fast, he mused. He reached the window and looked outside. That was strange, he thought. The sky was full of stars and the moon, though only half full, was bright enough for him to see the outlines of the village.

Something tugged at Dunsor. He wasn't quite sure what it was but something stirred deep inside his soul as the rumbling sound grew closer and closer. Then, off in the distance Dunsor saw an orange glow appearing. As the brightness grew near, it seemed to split off in several directions. It was then that the older farmer realized what had been nagging at his insides.

"Oh my god," he said silently.

He suddenly grew very awake. He ran to the far wall where his old war axe lay against the fire hearth. He snatched it up and headed for the door. By the time he reached the outside air the village was awake. Women screamed and men cursed at what they saw.

Dozens of riders appeared on the edge of West End. Their torches cast an eerie glow across the main thoroughfare as they raced their mounts through the village. A song of death had come from far away and it showed no mercy.

Men, women, and children were being cut down as they came from their homes in terror. Blades sang through the air and were answered by the grizzly sound of metal slicing through skin and bone.

Dunsor cast a hopeless glance to a small hill off to the side of the village. Their sole protection lay with the men of the small keep that stood atop the hill like a proud beacon. Dunsor knew though that it would be a futile fight. Their lord was gone in the capital of Brulan, two hundred and fifty miles to the southeast. That left the captain of the guard, Epstein and his men who at the best numbered a dozen.

Dunsor sensed something and turned. A rider was headed straight for him. The attacker raised a large sword for Dunsor but the older man had not only been a farmer. He charged the rider as fast as his old bones could carry him. Both swung their weapons at each other meeting in a shower of sparks. Dunsor jerked with the impact and fell to the ground. However he rolled with the connection and came up again on his feet. Pain shot through his body but he shook it off.

The attacker reeled his horse around and charged again. Dunsor stood there with both hands firmly gripping the handle of the axe. It had served him many years ago in his youth and to this day he kept the blades sharp. In one fluid motion the rider pulled the reins hard and slipped from the saddle. He swung his weapon in a series of arcs but Dunsor wasn't intimidated. He had faced this kind of man before and had come out on the winning end more times than not.

Dunsor growled at the man. "Come on you bastard!" he shouted. "You will see that I don't cower to your kind!" He spat at the man.

The attacker moved forward, his blade slicing through the air. The blades met again and the two danced in unison of swings. It was a simple exchange of attack, parry, and attack. It went on for several moments. Eventually Dunsor felt his strength slipping past. The man was younger than he was and all his years were starting to catch up with him.

Shouting in the distance ran through the air. Dunsor's eyes darted for a split second to see the defenses of West End trying desperately to keep the attacking force at bay. He realized too late that his decision to look was his downfall. There was a loud yell and Dunsor turned back to the problem at hand. But it was too late. His parry slipped and he felt the cold hard steel cross his chest.

Dunsor fell to his knees, his body wretched in pain. Then the world began to grow cold as he slowly slipped to the ground. By the time he was looking up into the clear starry night, one of the leaders of West End was dead.

And the killing continued.

Chapter One

Father Rurik Ironside's head was lowered in silence as he walked the narrow path of woods behind the slaughtered village of West End. Out of six-hundred men, women, and children there were about half of that left. The raiders had killed or maimed everything they had seen. The survivors were confused and scared as their village was decimated beyond belief. They wondered what would happen for them as their protection from Brightblade Manor was cut down within minutes of trying to defend the village. Without them there was no protection unless they provided it on their own which Rurik doubted they could. As church bishop for the northern land he felt it lay on his broad shoulders to find help where he could. Father Becca would tend to the needs of West End the best he could but only God knew the future of the village.

Rurik walked his path, his mind racing at what to do. He could ask Redmere for help but it was doubtful the lord there would send it. The knights at his garrison were greedy individuals who cared little about their honor nor the code with which the Etarian Knights were famous for. He had an inkling of what to do but whether or not he could convince the young man was another task. In reality, it was the young man's duty to assume command of Brightblade manor for it now belonged to him. But the young Kaylen's past was troubled and this worried Rurik.

The path wound down a small hill among the colorful fall colors. Shades of yellow, orange, and brown hung along the trees, separated by the green pines of the land. At the bottom of the hill Rurik turned to another path that paralleled a slow moving creek. It was here where he would find the boy, sitting on an outcropping of rock. As he approached he was relieved to find Kaylen exactly as he predicted. Hearing his approach on the leaves, the boy looked up and gave a grim smile. Rurik was relieved that he hadn't run away, but then again where could he run away to? There wasn't another village for miles and Redmere a day and a half away.

Rurik walked up to the rocks and sat down with a heavy grunt. The dwarf kept silent as he let the minutes tick away. Finally he turned to the young man. "Are ye okay?"

Kaylen nodded. "Yes Father. Just startled as is everyone else."

The dwarf nodded. "Aye. It is startling. However, as the tides roll in and out of the sea, life does go on. This is why I am here."

Kaylen arched an eye.

"You're needed," said Rurik. "The time has come for you to take your place in life Kaylen. I've prayed about it all morning and each time the Lord God replies the same. You need to assume the command of Brightblade Manor."

Kaylen shook his head. "No Rurik. I can't do that and I won't' do that."

"You must," protested the priest, "It is your duty to assume control. You are the son of Augustus Brightblade.'

"No, I'm the 'bastard son' of Augustus Brightblade," stated Kaylen. He stared out across the creek his mind a thousand places other than northern Kesh. "My father has other children who are more equipped to take control than me."

"No he doesn't. Gerard has his own manor to take care of. As far as Gisela, she would gladly give the right to you in order to keep it in the family."

"And Isabella?" asked Kaylen.

"Aye Isabella," hissed Rurik. He had forgotten about the evil wench, God forgive him. Augustus' wife and the mother to Kaylen's half-siblings, Isabella Brightblade was nothing more than a social snob trying to climb the social ladder of Kesh society. She knew about Kaylen and in fact it was her idea to keep him at West End and away from the capital. She was a conniving woman who used Augustus' military status as a stepping stone to her own power.

"Forget Isabella," insisted Rurik. "She is far away from here and has no interest in Brightblade Manor here in West End. These are your people Kaylen. They all like you and will accept you as the rightful heir."

"And if they don't? They know I'm illegitimate to my father."

"Believe me they will. They need a leader."

"Do you really think my father will appoint me?"

Rurik looked toward the direction of the village. "I really don't think he has a choice."

Augustus read the report with sadness. Three hundred citizens of Kesh wiped out in a single blow. What made matters worse it happened on his lands to the north. The closest help would be Lord Ridley in Redmere but that was a gamble all its own. Ridley's men were of the shadowy kind and they were under constant surveillance by Etarian Knights to make sure they were behaving as best they could. Augustus laid the small message down. It had been delivered by messenger pigeon early in the morning which meant the attack was about two days ago. By now the dead would be buried and Bishop Ironside would be waiting for his word regarding his son. He looked up with the cool grey eyes of someone who'd had years of experience, yet this decision was a difficult one for sure. His hand reached out for a quill and wrote the response for his aide.

"Have this sent to West End at once Thomas," he said. "And then come back with two three scribes at dusk. We are going to have a long night ahead of us."

"Yes my lord," replied Thomas. He pocketed the small message and then left the room.

Augustus Brightblade stood and walked to the single window of his study. He pushed open the rafters and stared out across the city streets of Brulan, the capital of Kesh. Among the white-washed buildings covered with red tiles, he watched as the population went about their daily business. Men and women conversing as they packed the markets, children giggling as they played, dogs barking off in the distance, all unaware of the protection that was required to keep their lifestyle comfortable. The domed stone cathedrals where mass was held by a variety of religious sects, glowed in the morning as the sun bounced off the smoothly polished marble.

As a leading commander of the Etarian Knights, his duty was to keep the enemies of Kesh at bay and for the last twenty five years he had done so. He had risen in rank quickly after successful campaigns in the deserts of Zakistan and the forested region of Germatica. Now, he commanded the 2nd Legion of Etarian Knights and their men at arms. One thousand men in total and based here in Brulan. His days comprised of reports and meetings. If he was lucky he could take in an afternoon ride to watch his men go over their daily practice of military training. His large frame was decorated with the traditional dark blue breeches, a pull over blouse and a vest of dark blue cotton. Upon his vest lay the medals of his campaigns. With his gray haired neatly trimmed and dressed sharply, he was a massive figure that demanded attention and respect.

There was a knock on the door and he turned.

"Enter," he said gruffly.

The door to his office snapped open and a thinner man, dressed in the same style of uniform walked in. His face was narrow and long while his hair was black with streaks of gray. He nodded briefly to Augustus.

"Lord Harper," said Augustus.

"What's going on Augustus?"

"My manor in West End was attacked. Half the village was murdered."

"My god," replied Harper. He slumped into a cushioned chair before Brightblade's desk. He ran a hand through his hair. "Do we know who did it?"

Augustus shook his head. "No. Nothing yet. Probably raiders but right now I barely know anything."

"I will talk to the senate and arrange your leave so you can handle this."

"I'm in the process of that," said Augustus. He sighed heavily. "I won't need to take leave though. My place is here with my legion."

"But what of Brightblade manor in West End?"

Augustus stared at him. It took a moment but Harper finally realized what he was talking about. They had been friends for a long time and although Harper was his superior, the two held a bond that was tighter than a husband and wife could ever achieve.

"Are you serious?" asked Harper.

Augustus nodded. "Yes. I don't really have a choice now do I? Besides, Kaylen is the logical choice wouldn't you agree?"

Harper sighed. "I don't know the answer to that Augustus. What do you think the senate will say?"

"It doesn't really matter. They have no say in it to be truthful. Brightblade manor is my property and I have the right to defend it how I see fit. Kaylen is my son Alvin and he has the right to take over the manor if I see fit. In fact, word has already left my office that he is to do so."

Harper nodded. He didn't really agree with his friend but he could see that Augustus was determined to carry this through. "Word will get out you know."

"So let it. West End is far out on the frontier Alvin. No one will care."

The two sat for a moment looking at each other. Both were thinking the same thing and waited for the other to bring it up. Augustus wasn't going to say it for sure; though he knew it more than anyone it was true. But he would have to deal with it. After all, she was his wife and the thought of his illegitimate heir controlling his property on the other side of the country would bring out her wrath for sure.

"What do you think she will do?" asked Harper after a few moments.

Augustus shrugged. "Don't know. Whatever happens I'll handle it."

Harper nodded. "Okay. If you need anything let me know. Please keep me posted on this too. I want to know if this was a random attack by bandits or something else."

Augustus nodded. He turned away and looked out the window again but he didn't see a beautiful day, he just saw an uncertain future for the seed of his weakness.

Chapter Two

Kaylen stood in silence as the pyres slowly burned away the ashes of the last group of bodies. He said a silent prayer to God asking that their souls find peace and rest in the darkness of death. He wasn't that close with God but somehow he hoped that the deity would at least hear his prayer and would grant him this one wish.

As the smoke floated lazily in the air Kaylen turned back to look at West End. The once peaceful village was in ruin. Several of the buildings were either gone or destroyed beyond repair. He didn't know who had survived and those that did he wondered whether or not they would stay or move on to start their lives somewhere else. On the small hill above West End sat the quiet manor where the Captain of the Guard and his men once lived. Now, he would be in charge.

Kaylen started walking up the hill toward town. Despite being half full it was rather quiet this morning. It could have been the weather, fall rains were coming every few days and the air held a perpetual coolness to it. Or, it could have been as he thought. Maybe the citizens were ready to leave.

"It's yours now," said a deep gruff voice.

Kaylen turned to see Father Rurik Ironside walking the street. The dwarf was doing his best to smile as he spread his arms wide. "Just think, Kaylen Brightblade is about to be christened a knight of the Etarian Order and be given control over all of West End." He chuckled as he slapped Kaylen on the back.

"Mmm," hummed Kaylen. "Not much to it I'm afraid. To be honest Rurik I don't know if this is a good idea."

"It's the only idea Kaylen. You are the son of Augustus Brightblade. You are the rightful heir."

"Maybe what's left of the village won't want me? Did you ever think of that?"

The dwarf nodded. He took Kaylen by the arm and they walked the streets. He led the young man through the main road and to a small corral where the animals of the city were usually kept. Kaylen's eyes grew large as he found out why the village was so quiet. Everyone who was left was gathered along the corral. They all turned to him as he was guided in.

He looked upon their faces and noticed the weariness, the lack of hope, and the weary faces of people who were just plain scared. Some of the women shed tears as they thought of lost husbands who had tried in vain to save the town. He took in their eyes, eyes that looked to him to restore something, anything at all really, so that they could begin the process of healing.

Rurik led him to a small area before the gathered crowd. Kaylen felt something firm on his shoulders and he soon found himself being forced to the ground before the priest. He knew what was happening but didn't feel worthy of what it meant. Why was this happening? He was young and inexperienced. What possible good could he hope to achieve?

From his kneeling position Kaylen watched as Rurik looked to the crowd. The priest held his hands out. "People of West End may I have your attention! A great travesty has fallen upon our fair village. We know not the intentions of God but for some reason he has allowed this to happen to us. We must look upon one another and comfort our neighbors. This is a test for us and our community. I urge you to not leave our town. I beg you to stay and rebuild to show the world that West End lives and will once again prosper."

There were tears of sadness. Tears of hope.

Rurik approached Kaylen. From one of the onlookers he took a sword. He laid the blade on Kaylen's head. "By the powers invested upon me from God and your own father Augustus Brightblade, I now christen you Lord Kaylen Brightblade, Knight of the Etarian Order, and now the protector of Brightblade Manor and of

West End of the country of Kesh. Now, rise a knight and fulfill your duty."

Despite the conditions of West End, her citizens found some sort of strength to send a round of cheers through the morning air. The echoes of their voices burned deep in Kaylen's soul and he shivered at the position given him.

Kaylen stood up. He let his eyes focus on the crowd and their faces. He would remember them each for they were now his responsibility. He swallowed hard. He looked to Rurik.

"I need your help Rurik," said Kaylen. "You know the survivors here. I need some sort of council. Have them assembled at the manor tonight. We need to put our town back together."

Kaylen nodded to the crowd and then took his leave. He had a lot of work to do and didn't really have a clue as to what to do. He walked slowly, his mind in deep thought.

West End was on the outskirts of the Kesh frontier and there would be little if any help from Brulan. He was sure his father would send something or someone to provide some sort of help but when it arrived he did not know. Fall was here which was good in some aspects of life. The crops were harvested and the granaries were full after a good season. With the population cut in half the people, his people, would not likely have to worry about food for the winter. Men, women, and children all helped to clean the city up from the attack but many were still in a dour mood. Several thatch covered buildings were gone, but they could be replaced as time went on. The stone and timber structures, although damaged would provide adequate protection from the elements. If there was any problem that Kaylen could see it was protection.

Kaylen kept to the path that led up to his home. Despite its modest size, Brightblade Manor was a scene of security in this part of the country. It was built over a hundred years ago by one of his father's ancestors. Made of stone from The Dead Peaks, it was reinforced over the years by thick timber and plaster. The sides were tall, nearly twenty feet. One tower jutted from the southwestern wall, spiraling another thirty feet from the top of the rampart. Fifty feet from the ground, it gave a good view of the surrounding lands. The inside of the fortress was complete with barracks, a small stable, and a tiny garden to provide fresh vegetables in the summer time.

Kaylen walked to the hall of the manor. It was small for a stronghold but with the warriors now dead it seemed to be too large. There was a large table and sitting arrangements for a dozen people against the far wall. A large hearth against the opposite side of the room provided heat that stifled the interior but would feel good when the winter snows came.

"Dammit," he swore. He fought to hold back the tears that hid behind his blue eyes. Kaylen had no clue as to what to do first. He had to protect what was left of West End but he had no inclination on how to do that.

"Are you okay my lord?" asked a sweet voice.

Kaylen turned at the interruption. Before him was the female servant of the house. She was a few years older than him which put her around twenty four summers old. Riva was a stunning beauty with long braided hair the color of rust. Her oval face bore smooth creamy skin that normally caused him to keep his eyes on her more than normal. He felt a stirring when he saw her and if she had any clue about his thoughts, she never let on.

"Please don't call me that Riva," he said. "We've known each other for ten years now and used to spend our time running around the creeks and fields of this place. We're alone and no one will know that you call me by my name."

"But your status has changed," she commented. "You are born from a knight and therefore you are considered royal to your kinsmen. You know this to be true."

"But I'm a bastard son," he retorted. "So much that my father and that bitch he's married too kept me out of the capital where I wouldn't be an embarrassment."

"You're not an embarrassment Kaylen. I've seen the way your father looks at you when he's here."

Kaylen wished he was here now. Augustus came to West End perhaps once a year and then only stayed a few weeks to ensure everything was in order. He did spend a little time with Kaylen but it was always awkward and neither really knew what to say or do when they were together.

"I'm lost Riva," he sighed. "Our village has been decimated. How am I supposed to protect the remainder?"

"You will find a way Kaylen. I have faith in you."

"Then you are the only one," he said in disgust. "I doubt if anyone believes that I can protect them from something like this again."

"They will. You are their hope and they will look to you for advice in the coming years. You must provide that for them."

He sighed again. He looked at the fire and watched the glowing embers of flame lick around the logs. What was he going to do?

"Bishop Rurik will help you," she said. "He adores you, you know that. You can trust in his word."

Kaylen looked at her. He gave a small smile and she returned it in kind causing his stomach to rumble as it did so many times before. Doubts were still there but Riva was right. Rurik would help him, she was right there. But it was a long road before him and somehow the nagging thought of his past kept him in wonder.

Chapter Three

Night fell and the citizens of West End settled in four days after the attack. It was a peaceful evening and a chill at come down from the mountains and spread across the rolling hills and plains of Kesh. Fires were lit and the town slowly began to return to normal as best as it could. Up on the hill the fortress hall was coming to life as Bishop Rurik Ironside assembled the members of town thought to be the next leaders, banning Kaylen's approval of course.

The newly appointed knight took his position at head of the large table. A variety of cheeses, bread, and honey were arranged so the visitors could enjoy a small meal as they discussed the future of the village. Copper tankards were filled with wine and everyone sat back in wait as their newly appointed leader gathered his thoughts.

"Thank you for coming gentlemen and ladies," said Kaylen. His voice was dry from nervousness and he took a moment to take a drink to help him. When he had cleared his throat the best he could, he nodded to them again. "Sorry. I'm a little nervous at this."

"Take your time Lord Brightblade," said a beefy sized man. Edwin Delapost reached out and touched the young man's arm with a meaty paw. He gave the lad a reassuring pat and a weak smile. "We have all evening to discuss things."

"Thank you Edwin," said Kaylen. He was unsure of the man as he knew little about the personal lives of these individuals. He was sure Rurik was well informed and would fill him in after the meeting.

"Now," continued Kaylen. "I need to know what exactly we have here so I can prepare accordingly." He turned to Rurik and addressed him in his official title. "Bishop Ironside, what is the extent of people left in our community?"

Rurik lowered his eyes for a brief second, taking in notes scribbled on a piece of parchment. When he looked up his face was somber as he gave his report. "West End has lost a great number of people. As of a census this morning, we have two-hundred seventy men from the ages of twenty thru sixty years old. The number of women in that age range is one hundred forty-five, and the number of children under twenty years of age is fifty-seven. That gives us a total population of four hundred and seventy-two."

Kaylen swallowed hard and nodded. It was a mighty blow to them. A mixture of disgust, sadness, and just pure anger flowed through his veins and for the first time he felt like he needed to do something to avenge their deaths, but that would happen in time. For now, the prosperity of West End had to be put in place.

"Can we expect Brulan to answer our call for aide?" asked a slender man with deep eyes.

"That I don't know Solomon," replied Kaylen. "I'm sure my father will assist but I don't know when it will come or in what form."

Solomon Jarlson was a trader by nature. His store was damaged and it would be weeks before it would be able to open its doors to the public again. He shrugged his shoulders and sighed heavily. "We will never be the same again."

The room grew quiet, all in their thoughts. A quick glance from Rurik to Kaylen brought the young man back to the task at hand.

"Yes we will," said Kaylen. "West End may have been attacked but we will recover from this. It may take time but our village will overcome this event."

"Who says it won't happen again?" asked a voice from the edge of the table. Willow Guthrie was an elderly but harsh woman who ran the Black Fawn, one of West End's inns. From what he had known she was a tough old bird who took shit from no one. If only she were younger and a warrior she would have been a good protector of the village.

"We're working on that," Kaylen assured the gathering. "Right now I need to call on the militia to help with things around here. Winter is approaching and I would like to offer a dozen of them full time positions within my household."

"That might be tough," said a small but well-rounded man. "As the militia was hit hard during the attack. We could maybe pull together twenty men who are strong enough to do it. The problem here is that they have no experience."

"I can train them," snorted Rurik. "You can get out there as well Gabriel and maybe work some of that fat off your bottom."

Everyone took a moment to laugh and bring some sort of goodness to the situation at hand. Rurik winked at the man, who returned the gesture with a smile.

"I will see what I can do," replied Gabriel. He turned to Kaylen. "You said a full time offer. How much are we talking about?"

So this is what it came too, thought Kaylen. The safety of West End rested on the thickness of his coffers, which by his account not the best in the world. Still, he had done the figuring during the afternoon and knew what he could afford and what he could not. "Three gold crowns a month," he said.

Gabriel threw his hand in the air and groaned. This was followed by a few others around the table, most of them citizen leaders and businessmen that had survived. "Three crowns a month? My 'lord' that will not be enough to get anyone to volunteer for your offer. Surely even you know that?"

"What would you have me do Gabriel? I can't afford to hire mercenaries nor do I really think you want me to do that."

Edwin raised a hand toward the younger but equally stout man in the middle. "It's okay Gabriel." He turned back to Kaylen and gave a smile.

Kaylen didn't know what it was but it seemed to be a little on the sly side and immediately his guard was up. "You have something to say Mr. Delapost?"

Edwin chuckled. "I would like to offer my help in this Lord Brightblade. I can supplement the offer by two a man. That would be five crowns a month per man. I can say, do this for what, maybe a year? That would give you time to arrange for proper protection from Brulan and to also put funds toward rebuilding the village."

Kaylen eyed him carefully. "In return?"

Edwin continued to smile, still sending a vile feeling through the young knight. "We can discuss that later. It's not important right now."

Kaylen thought for a moment, and then sighed. He saw no choice. He had to have a permanent guard force assigned to the stronghold to protect both his assets as well as those of the rebuilding village. He was somewhat reluctant but he gave a nod in agreement. Once this was done, he watched as the large man turned back to his counterpart.

"Does this suffice Gabriel?" asked Edwin.

Gabriel seemed to think about it for a minute and then finally nodded. "Aye. That will suffice. I think I can gather some men to volunteer for that."

The rest of the meeting was filled with discussion regarding the rebuilding of the village and the upcoming winter. They would have plenty to do regarding repairs and mending the damage caused by the raiders. Rurik decided to send Father Becca to Redmere to discuss the trade that frequented the town and village. They would be an important part in rebuilding West End and he knew that the priests there would be more than willing to help.

After the meeting broke up Kaylen found himself tired and worn out from the negotiations with his new town council. From now on they would have an active part in conversations around the village, though the real authority and decision making would be left to him. He sat with Rurik at the hall table finishing off their tankards of wine.

"Well?" asked Kaylen.

"Thought it went fairly well," grunted Rurik downing a healthy quantity of wine.

"So who should I worry about here Rurik? I know they're all not going to work with me to benefit the village. I'm sure some have alternative motives."

The dwarf thought for a moment. "They all have agendas Kaylen," he said. "I think most of them are trustworthy enough. Little concerned about Edwin to be honest. He's going to help you out financially but I would be cautious around him. He's not going to do anything for free."

"What about Gabriel?" asked Kaylen. He man seemed to be a little reluctant about the salary of the guards. He had little choice and even little money until help came from Brulan. Just how trustworthy would they be? He'd need Rurik's decision on this because it would be the dwarf doing the training.

"I don't know," replied Rurik. He finished his mug before sitting in quiet twirling it in his hands. "I'll have to see. There's something about him that makes me uneasy."

Kaylen nodded. At least they were on the same page as far as that was concerned. A yawn broke free reminding him how tired he was and how it would be this way for some time to come.

"Come on lad," said Rurik. "Off to bed with you. Tomorrow we will begin to redefine who you are and what your duty is."

Kaylen chuckled. "You're going to push me, aren't you?"

Oskar stood up. "You have no idea boy," he said as they locked eyes. Kaylen stopped his grin when he realized the old dwarf wasn't even amused at the attempted joke.

Chapter Four

One of the most beautiful cities in the world was Brulan, capital of Kesh. Located along the Sebren River, it was a major trading center in the central part of the continent and drew people from all walks of life. The city was home to merchants and a variety of people working in trades or crafts. Carpenters, cobblers, butchers, bakers, physicians, vendors of prepared food, and all sorts of other people made their living from the streets of the capital and the surrounding villages outside the city walls.

Brulan was divided into several districts according to social status. Aristocrats from the Senate and high profile businessman lived apart from the others among grand marbled estates with manicured gardens and clean streets. Apart from these came the Academic District where spiraled churches competed with each other and where institutions of learning and training all gathered. Apart from that Brulan was like any other city although her citizens enjoyed a serene atmosphere. Jutting out from the city in nicely arranged roads, homes with baked red roof tiles jutted out in every direction. Here was where the majority of citizens lived. Of course, the market and shipping district wasn't as appealing due to the heavy trade, but it was still comfortable to live in.

On this crisp fall morning, Atticus Bane walked the streets with a lowered head. Walking along the cleaned streets of the High District, he felt out of place among the richer of Kesh society. Few citizens were out in the early fall morning. Those that were out among the chill were dressed with thick woolen cloaks and were in deep conversations with each other. With his head lowered they paid little attention to him. For him that was good. Someone with his reputation would undoubtedly raise some concern to the local authorities. His life was full of adventure and unsavory characters of whom many wanted him dead. To have Brulan's security detachment looking into his business wasn't something he really wanted nor did any of his potential clients.

Atticus was a medium sized man with long dark hair. He was neither handsome nor ugly, just a plain looking man showing his age of forty some odd years. As an assassin by trade, his body did wear the scars of his profession but he wore them proudly. Perhaps if he had any negative attributes visible it was a disfiguration of a nose that had been broken many times. Normal people seemed to either ignore him or go about their way allowing him a wide berth. Regardless of what they did, they didn't bother this agile but powerful man.

He had walked the streets of Brulan since a little past dawn. He took a variety of routes that took him past the shipping docks, the merchant square, and the common area. If he was being followed the person had to be dammed good because Atticus was an expert at concealment and he hadn't seen a thing since leaving the inn. Satisfied that no one was trailing him, he had worked his way into the heart of Brulan's wealthiest families. He followed track the same as he had done in the lower districts. Left, right, and then left again. Always keeping track of his intended target, Atticus backtracked several of his routes until he came to the place he was looking for, The Gilded Goose.

Setting off a side road and positioned at an angle in a corner, "The Goose" as it was known, was a brown two-storied structure with a gabled roof. Going inside, Atticus could only imagine the smugness of the patrons inside. When he saw them his thoughts were verified. Although it was morning the place was filled with finely clothed men and women gathered about the tables. The smell of warm fruited pastries filled the air with a sweet aroma of cherries and apples hustled about by servants that were more richly dressed than him. Atticus looked about and found the person who had requested his service sitting against the far wall. He walked over to her slowly. His nervous eyes searching the room for hidden dangers. Seeing none, he sat on a smoothly carved bench across from her.

Isabella Brightblade was a thin well-dressed woman in her late fifties. Despite her age she was finely made up as most women with money tended to do. Her graying hair was finely combed and tied up. Her face, though a little wrinkled, still showed some sign of beauty that was probably adored in her younger years. She gave a quaint, yet devious smile at him. She said nothing, even when a waitress came and took his order. Atticus ordered red wine and despite ordering it watered down, he detected a hint of disgust on her face.

Atticus looked around. It was a charming place if a person was into that sort of atmosphere. High beamed ceilings held together bright cream colored walls where oil painting and tapestries hung to bring in a homey relaxed atmosphere. He thought it was ironic that he, a hired killer, sat here with one of the elite of Kesh society. If anything, it didn't bother Isabella to be seen with a ruffian even if he was smartly dressed today. That worried him.

When the waitress returned with his drink, Atticus thanked her and took a healthy sip. It was warm and definitely watered down but he enjoyed the same. With a small chill outside the liquor warmed his body some. "Good wine," he said.

"I find it hard that someone can drink so early in the morning," replied Isabella with sarcasm.

Atticus shrugged. "When your body has been abused as much as mine you have to take whatever works to keep it going."

"I find a good tea does the same thing."

Atticus snorted. This woman was a social bitch for sure. The upside to that was that she probably had money to spend. "So, since we're obviously not here to talk about the pleasures of society maybe you can tell me why we are here."

Isabella looked around nervously. Atticus caught her look and wondered what she was up to. He had offered a more secluded environment but for some reason she had picked the The Goose. Maybe she didn't want to be seen in such a raunchy environment or maybe she was just scared to go out of the high class district. Anyway, it was business now so he gave her a few moments to get settled.

"I want you to know that this is the first time I've done something like this," said Isabella. "I don't want you getting the wrong idea about me."

Too late, thought Atticus.

"Anyway," she continued. "I feel as if I can't trust anyone in Brulan anymore and had to step outside my boundaries if you must know."

Atticus shrugged. He could care less as long as he got paid for his troubles. "So, why did you call on me?"

"I have a delicate situation that I need handled. It's been going on for a long time now and I'm tired of it."

Of all things, Atticus thought. Was this another jealous wife killing? He hated those and wished the courts of Kesh would allow divorce to avoid him of killing some pour soul just because he couldn't take his wife's bitching anymore. "You'd be surprised how many times I've heard that before," he told her. "So what is it? Husband cheating on you? You want him put under the blade?"

Isabella's mouth dropped open. It took a moment but she regrouped herself. "No," she spat. "Even though I would like to do it for what shame he's brought to our family."

"I see," said Atticus. "Who is this person?"

"It's the new Lord of Brightblade Manor in West End."

Atticus arched his eyes. "A family member?"

Isabella shook her head. "No. Not from mine anyway. The new lord is my husband's bastard son."

Ah, thought Atticus. A family dispute taken too far. It wouldn't be the first time and it probably wouldn't be the last, though he was leery when it came to doing this. Sometimes the wrong person got killed and the worse one was left standing. Inside he cursed himself for starting to have a conscious. It wasn't a good thing to have one of those in his chosen career. But maybe it was a sign to start thinking about retirement.

"Let me guess," he said to her. "You don't want him to tarnish your family reputation."

Isabella nodded. "Very good Mr. Bane. You can see the predicament that I'm in."

"And your children? I'm sure they're suffering because of his recent promotion."

Something triggered inside Isabella. "My children are none of your concern Mr. Bane. They have nothing to do with this so leave them alone."

My, thought Atticus, the woman was feisty when it came to family values and loyalty. It was obvious this new lord was an embarrassment to her but to go and kill him? Despite his youth he was bound to have those loyal to him.

"Is he a terrible lord?"

She shrugged. "Who knows what he will be? I don't really care. I just want him removed from my property and sent back to the streets where he and his mother came from."

So there we have it, he thought. She actually wants revenge against her husband but was too scared to do it. A young lord without any experience wasn't much of a challenge and he was sure the leaders here in the capital would turn their eye on the whole situation, if they hadn't done so anyway. The only obstacle, if any, would be the boy's father.

"It's going to cost you," said Atticus. He looked at her wardrobe and figured he deserved to get as much as he could from her. "Ten shillings. Half now, half when the job is done."

"Ten shillings! I could buy a small army with that!"

"Then maybe you should. Makes no difference to me."

Isabella snorted. She took a look around again. Satisfied she wasn't being seen she reached into the folds of her dress and took out a small leather purse. After counting out the coins, she slid them across the table. "No mistakes Mr. Bane. I don't want this coming back on me."

"Don't worry," replied Atticus with a smile. "After this I don't think I want to show my face again in Brulan."

Of course, that was a lie.

Chapter Five

Two months had gone by and the village of West End had begun to return to normal. The pain and hurt of the previous attack was still there but like everything in life, it had its purpose and the world moved on. The buildings were repaired as the first snow came and everyone seemed to settle in for the normal routine of winter. It was a slack time of the year for most. Animals still had to be looked after but many of the community farmers took this time of season to mend harness and plows in preparation for the spring planting season. There wouldn't be a rush so they took their time and enjoyed long days of conversation with each other while they worked. The women also gathered for gossip as they spun and wove material for clothes. Children played and learned to help their families as everyone had done for hundreds if not thousands of winters before.

For Kaylen things were a little bit different. His days and those who now served as the guardsmen of Brightblade Manor were long and hard. Rurik had called on the aide of his cousin Oskar Dankil a boisterous dwarf who was an expert in fighting. He, along with his elf friend Kith Lightwood, ran the men hard day and night in fighting skills and battle tactics. Constantly they had drilled in every type of weather or condition that the two warriors could think of. At night, Rurik would spend on Kaylen's religious needs. To be an Etarian Knight, one had to make peace and have faith in the Gold Almighty. After a couple of months, Kaylen felt more disciplined than he ever had before. Still, when it came to making his peace with God, well that was a different matter. For some reason his past continued to haunt him and until he settled that account, he feared there would be no peace and understanding with God.

So on a cold lonely night, Kaylen knelt before the cross in West End's lone little church. He had his head bowed and tried to pray but could not find the words to say. He wanted to do good, wanted to help these people, but felt he was unworthy. After all, he was the bastard son of an Etarian Knight. Who could possibly love him? His mother was dead, his father only a figure in his life once or twice a year if at all. Sometimes he wished his father would have left him on the streets and never brought him to Kesh or Brulan. It would have been better off, he figured. After all, he was kept away from so called family that he had in Brulan. He knew that wicked woman Isabella didn't care for him. Why should she though? He wasn't her son. He wasn't a full sibling to Gerard and Gisela, so why should they care as well? His heart was heavy with emotions of sadness, hate, and confusion. Why would God, if there really was one, want him at all? For Kaylen Brightblade there were more questions than answers.

"Thought I would find 'ye here," said a gruff led voice.

Kaylen turned to see Oskar Dankil standing in the doorway. He was a stout warrior dressed in mail. His white grizzly looking hair jutted from underneath a horned helmet flowing in with his long beard. His face, from what Kaylen could see past the hair, was rosy from the winter wind.

"Hello Oskar," said Kaylen. "I was just praying."

"How's that going'?"

Kaylen shrugged. "Does it matter? God doesn't listen to me anyway."

"Aye sometimes it feels that way doesn't it."

Oskar sat down on a bench and folded his hands before him. "Ye are doing a good job lad. You know that don't ye?"

"Right now I don't know who I am Oskar. I have been thrust into a position that I know little about nor do I know if I can lead these men into battle if the need came to it. Now tell me, what kind of knight can say that?"

"A good knight if you ask me," replied the dwarf. "You stepped up when no one else would. The people here like you. West End seems to be rebuilding itself and not running away to another village or city. I think they would have to have some sort of faith in order to stick around."

"Maybe," said Kaylen. He got up and sat down next to Oskar. "So what about my men-at-arms? Do you think they're ready to provide protection to the village and manor?"

"Ah but no one will know until the moment of battle," said Oskar. "It will only be then that the true measure of courage is tested."

Kaylen sighed heavily. He rubbed the back of his neck trying to ease the stiffness that he was getting. Despite the physical training he was receiving the dealing with everyday matters of the village was beginning to run heavy on his mind as well. True, the citizens had done well without too much squabbling but he wanted to keep it that way. He was about to say something to Oskar when the door of the church burst open. In rushed Gabriel, breathing heavy from his chest.

"Lord Brightblade!" he said. "We have a problem."

Both Kaylen and Oskar arched their eyebrows in anticipation.

"What is it?" asked Oskar.

"O-orcs have crossed the Crooked Shallow! They've laid waste to a farm there, killing all but one. She managed to get into the village and warn them. By the time the villagers got there they were gone."

"Dammit," said Kaylen.

Crooked Shallow was ten miles to the north, right along the edge of Vespa. Kaylen doubted that the elves would put up with it. He turned to Oskar.

"I'll get Kith to go with you," said the dwarf rumbling toward the door as fast as his stout legs would allow. He turned back just as he was leaving. "Get your men Kaylen. Kith will go with you to help out. Remember our talk lad. This is your time."

Kaylen, Kith, and the small band of men at arms pulled up short of the hamlet of burning thatch homes. The young knight sat there for a moment in shock as flames burned what was left of the farming community.

"God has no mercy," muttered one.

"Quiet," hissed Kith. He was a normal sized elf with long black hair that was formed in several braids. He turned his horse around to quell the uneasiness of the beast. "God didn't do this, orcs did. You all remember that when we find them."

"Who said we're going after them?" asked Gabriel from his mount. "There is nothing we can do here now. Everyone is dead."

Kaylen felt all eyes look toward him. He hated this, he told himself. He was too young to be doing this and he silently cursed his father for putting him into this situation. Still, he felt anger for those freakish creatures behind this.

"I said so," said Kaylen through gritted teeth. He looked at the elf. "Well Kith where are they?"

The elf was a ranger and he knew more about tracking than anyone Kaylen had encountered. He led the party into the burning mess of ruined thatch and jumped from his horse. He looked to the ground, then around the area, and back to the ground again. Kaylen watched his ears twitch as Kith surveyed the surroundings. A minute later they were exiting the town and heading for a stream a hundred yards away.

Snow and mud flew through the air as sharp hooves beat with intensity at the ground. The party pulled to a stop at the edge of the creek and looked down upon a blood soaked patch on the ground. A female elf clutched a young child, both their eyes open and staring into the abyss.

Kaylen felt something deep inside him burn. It was like nothing he had ever experienced before. Complete rage consumed his soul and he cursed at nothing in particular. He saw nor heard nothing before him with the exception of his own heavy heartbeat. He felt his hand starting to shake but stopped it with a clenched fist.

"Find them Kith," said Kaylen. "Find them now."

Kith eyed Kaylen. The others couldn't see it but the elf's strong vision caught the slight tremble in the young man's posture. Something had sparked inside the knight and the elf knew that he would have to bring it up to Oskar or perhaps say something himself. But for now, he had to find the orcs. "I will," he replied softly.

For the next hour the party scoured the countryside hills and forests. This land was on the border between Kesh and Vespa, home of the elves. The woods were thick with trees but thanks to the time of season most had already dropped their leaves and it was easier to see. It wasn't until mid-day when Kith caught the strong scent of the orc clan. He led the group to a gully in a patch of forest thick with pine trees. The orcs were nestled in a small camp within the pine, obscured by the snow covered needles. A small fire blazed while a score of the creatures sat about drinking out of clay jars and examining their success of goods from the destroyed hamlet.

Kaylen slid from his saddle. His blood ran with fury as his sword came from its scabbard with a quiet hiss. He walked down the side of the gully, his eyes focused on the evil creatures before him. He had no idea if his men or Kith followed him, he could only hope that they were. But he was worried less about them as he was about wreaking havoc on those before him. As he approached, the orcs looked up from their loot. A loud howl echoed across the land as the horde all yelled in unison. Kaylen felt a chill run down his spine. He gripped the handle of his sword trying to get a natural feel. He swallowed hard as the moment of truth approached him in the form of a giant orc with a war axe.

The orc swung wildly and Kaylen sidestepped. He swung hard and felt the initial jolt as metal bent the flimsy armor that the orc wore. Once past the orcs defenses Kaylen felt the blade slip into the greenish flesh of the creature. The orc howled and dropped to his knees. Kaylen was about to go for another swing when two arrows ripped into the beast's chest sending him falling to the ground. Out of the corner of his eye he saw Kith reload his bow and gave a slight nod.

Yelling mixed with the orcs shouts grew into chaos as men joined in the battle. Steel met steel causing the air to fill with sparks of metal. Kaylen wanted to see how the others were fairing but there was no such luck. He turned just in time to parry a blow from an oncoming sword. The blow caused him to turn so he used the momentum and spun even further so that he came all the way around. His blade smashed into an orc leg. Kaylen pulled the sword back quickly and swung again. There was a sharp snap and the creature's head rolled away into the snow. By now, he felt the urge to vomit.

A flurry of movement caught Kaylen's attention. Coming in hard an orc slammed his sword toward Kaylen's head. The young knight parried and caught it on his own blade, feeling it scrape down the length of steel. The attacker kept coming, his intent lethal. Going on training and instinct, Kaylen thrust out his knife. The orc moaned and swatted a fist at his side. Kaylen felt a jarring impact. There was no pain yet, but he knew he'd been hit. Drawing a deep breath that made his injured ribs howl, Kaylen attacked, driving hard in a flurry of strikes that kept the orc too busy parrying to make any counters of his own. He kept going until he was almost chest to chest with the larger beast. His side throbbing a kettle-drum beat of agony, Kaylen rammed a knee into the orcs muscled belly. Leaping back as his opponent hissed in pain, the young man bellowed a battle cry. The orc looked up into his lunge with large grey eyes. Kaylen saw his opponents eyes widen slightly as he charged. Sighting down the length of his bloodied blade, the young knight pushed forward with all his might until the orc fell to the ground.

And then, all was quiet.

Chapter Six

The hall was quiet that night. As Kaylen moved his beef stew around in his bowl he took note of the three missing chairs sitting around the table. Three men, one of which was Gabriel, had left upon returning to the manor. He paid them what was owed and they left without saying a word. He was sure the others would leave as well but they put their weapons and armor away without a word being said. He had hoped that Gabriel would have taken over as Captain of the Guard but the young man didn't do well in battle and he had been the first to pack his belongings.

"You boys fought hard today," said Rurik. "Kith says that you all performed with valor and fought like warriors."

There were several nods but no one said a word.

"So what now Rurik?" asked Kaylen after a few moments. He pushed the remaining stew aside and reached for his cup of wine.

"That is up to you young Kaylen. Oskar and Kith are done with the training though they left instruction that it should be drilled several times a week throughout the winter. They will be leaving shortly, ye know? South before the heavy snows fall."

"Do you really think we're ready?"

"You are ready Lord Brightblade or they wouldn't be leaving. Now if you'll excuse me, I must tend to the church for a little while and be in my thoughts."

The men at arms sat in silence before finally starting talking about the day's events. They were happy that they had sought retribution on those responsible for attacking a village of Kesh. The fact that they were orcs were a little troublesome though because the orcs usually stayed in the mountains, and although they were close, the greenish creatures shouldn't have come this far south in winter.

"What now Lord?" asked one.

Lars Ulrich was a medium sized man with flowing hair. A native of Germatica, he had been in West End since a youth. He was a blacksmith by trade and was one of the best in the land. All through training he honed his skills and never complained as some had. He had fought well today and Kaylen was considering him for the new Captain of the Guard.

"We need to patrol the outer edges of our land," said Kaylen. "Lars I want you to set up a schedule somehow. Rotate it evenly and put me in it as well."

"But my lord you are the knight here. You shouldn't be involved in routine patrols. Let us take care of that."

Kaylen shook his head. "No. If I am to lead then I want to be involved in the boring routine work as well." This brought nods and grins of acceptance from the remaining men of his guard.

"Can we expect some sort of relief from Brulan?" asked another.

All Kaylen could do was shrug at Darius Pike's question. Pike was similar to Lars' size but with shorter darker hair. He had received a nasty cut across his face that was now stitched up. There was little doubt that he would carry a scar on his cheek the rest of his life.

"Father Rurik has received word that help is coming eventually but they are tied up in some political debate," said Kaylen.

"Bloody politicians. What is there to debate?"

If there was one flaw to Pike it was that he seldom knew when to keep his mouth shut. Good fighter, but he was a complainer as well. "We know how the senate can be Darius," said Kaylen. "So for right now we're the ones defending West End."

"Do you think they'll attack again?" asked Lars.

"I don't know," said Kaylen. "That is why I want to run these patrols. We are to scout and report anything that we find back here. We'll make the decision whether or not to take any retribution. I can't imagine the orcs coming down this far during the winter months. Hopefully they've learned their lesson for now."

The group stayed up for another few hours talking among themselves before breaking for the night. Kaylen refilled his wine cup and stood on his room balcony overlooking the cold night sky. Despite a heavy fur cloak wrapped around him he could barely keep warm. Yet, he stayed looking at the sleeping town below him. How did he get himself into this? One day he was the illegitimate son of a powerful officer of the Etarian Knighthood. He had been kept away from the capital to avoid embarrassment and grew up here in a lonely manor. He had never been expected to perform much even though the citizens here knew who he was. Now, he was thrust into protecting West End with little assistance from the capital or it seemed his father.

Kaylen felt something from behind and turned. Standing in the dim torchlight of his room was Riva. She was dressed in a long gown.

Her arms were folded tightly about her as she shivered.

"Good lord woman get inside before you catch cold," said Kaylen.

"I'm fine," she stated sternly.

Kaylen moved forward and slid his fur coat around her. "Take this. I can't have the lady of the house getting sick." He noticed her blushing as he bundled her up. He was much colder but wasn't going to show her. "What are you doing here?"

"Couldn't sleep," replied Riva. "My worries seem to keep me up at night."

"You shouldn't worry Riva. West End is safe."

"I know. But I worry about you too Kaylen. You've had to take on a great responsibility."

"I have there's no doubt about that. But apparently it's my job."

"Is it?"

Kaylen's eyes narrowed. "What do you mean?"

"I mean I don't think it's your job Kaylen."

"Well it is," he stammered. "I didn't ask for it but it was handed to me by Augustus

Brightblade, the rightful heir to Brightblade Manor."

Riva lowered her head. "I meant no harm Kaylen."

Kaylen felt a lump grow in his throat. He had always liked Riva. She was fun to be around and when she had taken over the cleaning and cooking duty he found he had more time with her than he ever dreamed of. Still, she didn't need to worry about him. He may not know what he was doing as far as the knighthood, but he had to grow up and maybe this was the way God had predicted it would be. He lifted her chin. "I'm sorry. I didn't mean to sound angry."

Riva held him close and let her tears flow. Only God knew how long they stood in each other's arms, both crying, both trying to find peace and reassurance in the far reaches of Kesh.

"What seems to be the problem Alvin?" asked Augustus.

"The senate is restricting you from sending in the army to West End," replied Lord Harper from a worried face. "I'm afraid there is little I can do."

"And why are they doing that? Are they just letting West End fall to the side? For God's sake Alvin,

West End is a summer home for my family and well within the boundaries of Kesh."

"But it's not an 'official' problem Augustus, you know that. Your report indicated it was nothing more than a band of raiders, and that is something the senate is not going to get involved in. For that you'll have to let the local authorities deal with the problem."

Augustus stood from the table and slammed a fist hard onto the table. Others in the tavern looked their way as nosy patrons usually did. Dissatisfied that it was nothing more than words they went back to their drinking and gambling. "The authority there was my Captain of the Guard who was cut down by these bastards!"

Harper looked up. "Sit down Augustus. We have much to discuss and it's not going to get done if you're standing up shouting at me like a little pup. Please, let's talk about this."

"Talk is getting really tiresome around here Lord Harper. Over two hundred people are dead. Does that really sound like a 'raid' to you?"

"Don't forget who sent Kaylen there in the first place. I warned you that he was too young to be handling things there."

Augustus looked around. He finally sighed heavily and eased back into his chair. "Look Alvin we have to do something. Why wouldn't the senate let me send an attachment of my troops to West End, even if it's just to look around?"

"They don't think it's anything to worry about Augustus. Like they said, that part of Kesh is full of unknown dangers. For all we know it could be renegade elves going mad or something."

The gray haired man chuckled at the comment. "I can't believe you would even consider that. The elves rarely come out of Vespa you know that Alvin. There is something more there. Something going on."

"And you have proof?"

"That's why I want men sent there. To get the proof we need to mobilize the army."

Harper started to say something but Augustus held up a hand. "Never mind. I don't feel like going around in circles with you over this. The senate has spoken its word and you're backing them on this."

"That's my job," said Harper.

Augustus pointed a finger at his friend. "No. That's not your job. Your job Alvin is the Commander of the Etarian Knights and the highest ranking general we have. You are in command of the army and now you're bowing to the will of a bunch of politicians for some unknown reason."

Harper grew tight lipped. He reached for his tankard and emptied it in one steady drink. When he finished he wiped the corners of his mouth and looked at Augustus. "There is a way. Lord Markel and his men are due to leave for Redmere the day after tomorrow to escort a dozen priests to the town. Maybe they can take a detour to West End. But they can't stay more than three days there looking around. Will that suffice?"

It was better than nothing, thought Augustus. He gave a quick nod. "It will. I will send word to Father Rurik in West End by nightfall." He stood up to leave but was stopped by his friend's tight grip. "You still have a lot to learn about the politics of Kesh my friend. Perhaps one day you will reach the point in your life when you'll need the senate."

"I doubt it," sneered August. And he walked out into the afternoon sunlight.

Chapter Seven

Atticus Bane stepped from the stirrups and slid off his mount. He had been on the road for more than several weeks working his way through the countryside of Kesh and visiting dozens of villages and hamlets. No one had heard of the young knight Kaylen Brightblade but they had heard of an attack on West End. Word was that a young man there had been appointed a knight in order to protect the village and that even though half of the population was killed, the village was slowly moving on with life.

So the young man had been given a promotion, thought Atticus. How quaint. He had eventually moved his way to the village at a snail's pace. Atticus wasn't new at this and he wanted to know everything about the land that he now traveled. He came upon the dead orcs several days after they had been slaughtered. What was left of them was being picked away by forest creatures and by carrion flying overhead. But he had seen enough to know that whoever had done this had done so with finely sharp weapons and precision attacks.

Atticus then worked his way north. The Death Peaks were a small mountain chain in the center of the continent and home to several clans of orc tribes that usually came out during the summer months. However, as he worked his way in and out of the mountain trails, he saw plenty of activity. Especially out of one tribe.

Vokar was a large greenish-gray beast with deep scars. His face was ragged and jagged from hundreds of fights that were accustomed among his race. His tusks, although yellow, were curved and pointed. He stared at the assassin through narrow eyes. He stood at the head of his tent, his leadership staff held firmly in his hand to show Atticus that he was the one in charge and that his word demanded respect and honor.

Nestled in the deep confines of a small gorge, the clan of Vokar was several hundred in number. Both male and female participated in battle though the young ones were tended primarily by their mothers or sisters. Their shelters were crude leather bound tents and lean to shelters that provided little protection from the elements. Not that it mattered to them for they were creatures of the outside and were used to the difficulties of living out in the open.

Atticus approached Vokar slowly. He held his hands wide showing respect and showing the orc leader that he carried no weapons in his hands.

"Who are you?" asked Vokar.

"My name is Atticus Bane," replied the assassin. "I am unfortunate in the fact that I bring terrible news to Vokar of the Ruddock Clan." The truth was Atticus hated orcs and he could care less if the young knight had killed a score of them.

Vokar grunted. He looked to another orc and muttered something Atticus couldn't understand. The younger orc moved forward and began to frisk the assassin. Luckily Atticus had removed a great deal of weapons from his body and came with only one short sword which was taken.

"Weapons will be returned when you leave," said the orc.

"What are you talking about?" asked Vokar. "Why are you here human? This is orc land."

Atticus nodded. "I understand great Vokar. May we talk in private?"

Vokar eyed him for several seconds. Finally he gave a grunt and waved him inside the tent. Atticus took a careful glance around and walked slowly inside. As the flap fell across the entrance the assassin almost gagged at the smell of orc body odor.

The quarters were tight but surprisingly comfortable looking. A pile of thick furs lay in one corner where two females lay sleeping. Vokar shouted and the two jumped to their feet and ran outside. Several small chests and casks lay against the back wall while a table held bits and pieces of meat and blackened bread. Vokar pointed to a small brazier where coals gave off a little but much welcomed heat.

"Sit," he said. He sat cross legged while Atticus sat down opposite him. They shared a wineskin of hard liquor before either spoke.

"What do you have to say to Vokar?" asked the orc.

Atticus coughed at the drink and put the cap back on the stopper. "Four days ago I found a score of dead orcs in a clearing at the base of The Death Peaks. They had been attacked and are now rotting in the fall rain."

"They are not from my clan," said Vokar. "All orcs in this clan are here. It is not my concern."

"Ah but that is the problem Vokar Ruddock. Those orcs may not be of your group, but the ones who killed them will be scouring your lands soon. They want revenge for the destruction of their village."

Vokar growled deeply. "What village?"

"West End I do believe. Word among the lands is that a young knight is now protecting the village. I heard this knight is rather reckless and thirsty for blood."

"Bah! I can handle an Etarian Knight. This knight is not a worry for me nor my clan."

"How do you plan on dealing with him?"

Vokar grunted. "Why are you asking many questions of me? Who are you?"

Atticus shook his head. "Just someone who is as worried as Vokar Ruddock about this knight."

The green beast arched his dark eyebrow. "Who said I needed your help? Why would you help orcs out?"

"I have my reasons," stated Atticus.

"Why should I trust you?"

Atticus smiled. "Because I can give this knight to you. Just think Vokar, if you were to take out this young man, then you can tell the rest of the clans in these mountains that you took revenge yourself. They would be in your debt."

Atticus waited while the orc pondered this. Orcs were strange in some aspects, he thought. Sometimes it took their brains a while to put things together while other times they were sharp as a whip. In his years it had always been that way and it would probably still be that way long after he was gone.

"Other clans would owe Vokar," the green monster finally said. "My men would be leading clan in area. The other clans would honor and have to pay tribute."

"Yes," replied Atticus. So there it was. No matter whether human or monster, the thought of power was an aphrodisiac that couldn't be ignored. "You will be a great clan leader Vokar. The masters of all the lands will know that you and your clan will rule the Death Peaks and they will tremble under the feet of you and your kin."

Vokar grunted. His lips turned up revealing his sharp tusks in a sort of grin. "Vokar will rule. Ruddock clan will rule by his side with iron fist. But Vokar still want to know answer to question. Why you help us?"

Atticus shook his head. "It is a personal matter. It has nothing to do with you or your clan."

"Your name?"

"Atticus Bane."

Vokar made a series of grunts as he rubbed his head with a massive green fist. "Vokar decides. Atticus may help Vokar's clan. But Vokar will watch. If you are lying to me I will kill you. Understood?"

Atticus nodded. He wouldn't have expected otherwise. It wasn't personal it was just the way the game was played. And right now Atticus was the one moving his pieces into action.

"You wanted to see me?" asked Kaylen.

Rurik had a small room that he used as his personal quarters and reading room. The priest was sitting at a table with scrolls laid out. Across from the priest sitting in a small backed chair was Edwin Delapost, the newly appointed mayor of West End, despite Kaylen's protests to Rurik.

"Ah Lord Brightblade," said Edwin. "How does your training go?"

"Training is training," he replied. "We prepare for the worst and there have been circumstances that have tried to break us but they have not done so."

"Good. Now comes the time to deal with other manners at hand I'm afraid. No such rest for a man leading West End back into the spotlight of the world."

Wow, thought Kaylen. This man had some dreams didn't he? West End would always be a village near the borderline with the elves. The latter wouldn't hurt them by any means. However, it also meant that the elves liked to be left alone unless their own lands were threatened. Kith was different, thought Kaylen, but he was with Oskar working on trade relations in Redmere right now. He wished that he could have gone with them but Rurik was adamant that he stay here. With the mayor sitting in the bishops quarters he was glad he listened to the old dwarf. His needs were still here.

"What are these other matters that you're referring to Edwin?" asked Kaylen. "Something other than protection perhaps?"

"Progress doesn't always mean going around picking fights Lord Brightblade."

"I wasn't aware I was picking fights."

"I didn't say you were. But we must discuss other things besides going out and taking down a group of orc raiders."

Kaylen's stomach turned tight. Rurik had warned him of Edwin and now he was starting to turn his true colors. Kaylen turned to the dwarf priest. "Rurik? You've always been honest with me and I expect a truthful answer now. What is he talking about?"

The dwarf shuffled about and for the first time in his life he thought he saw apprehension on his friend's face. "Edwin here has been talking to a few of the smaller villages regarding the upcoming summer harvest. Normally they bring their grain and goods here to market."

"I know this Rurik," stated Kaylen a little too sternly. "I'm not new to this village. What are you getting at?"

Edwin grunted. "Forgive Father Ironside my lord for he doesn't really know the fine details of business. What he is trying to tell you is that I've been having informal meetings with others regarding the tariffs we impose on them for bringing their goods to market."

Kaylen felt his face go flush. "And?"

"Some of the other businesses in West End and I feel that since our village was practically destroyed we have suffered extreme financial hardships. We feel that we must increase the cost of allowing them to do business here."

"Which they do Edwin," said Kaylen. "They pay a fair wage upon setting up their booths at market. How much do you and your cronies expect to raise the cost?"

"Well," replied Edwin, "the normal cost is five copper pieces per booth. In the past we feel that was a fair amount."

"And now?"

For a brief second Edwin paused before replying. "We are now asking two silvers."

Kaylen shook his head. "No. I won't allow it."

"You won't allow it?" asked Edwin. "I hardly think you're in a position to disagree. In fact, according to Kesh law you can't. The mayor and businesses of each village are allowed to elect their own laws."

"These are my lands," swore Kaylen.

"On the contrary Lord Brightblade they are not," grunted the stout businessman. He pointed a beefy finger in a general direction. "Your land, Brightblade Manor, is sitting on a hill overlooking the town. That is your land, not the entire town of West End."

"Which I protect."

"Correct. You protect, you do not own. The Etarian Knights may be nobles but they are still citizens of Kesh and the laws of this land are pretty firm. We have the right to increase our prices."

Kaylen shook his head. "This is wrong Mr. Delapost and you know it."

Edwin shrugged. "Maybe, maybe not. But my job is to make sure West End prospers and becomes something important again."

"But we are doing that slowly, can't you see?"

"What I see Lord Brightblade is that you wouldn't even be able to protect this town without my financial assistance, is that not true? Why are you fighting me against this?"

"People will make the extra journey to Redmere. Did you ever think of that?"

"Yes, but at two days extra in travel both ways? No, they'll complain but they'll come here and we all know it."

"I'm warning you Edwin, if people do come here they're going to be mad as all hell. If we're not careful, brawls could break out."

Edwin nodded. "It could happen. But then we'll call the militia out to deal with it."

"Militia?" asked Kaylen. "What militia? We had to bring them into service to help take care of the orcs or whatever else is out there."

Rurik, who had been quiet the whole time, finally grumbled something. Kaylen hadn't caught it and turned to ask him what he had said but Edwin took his position and made the remark instead.

"We have a new militia," said the businessman. "Men who will handle the internal strife, if any, within town."

Kaylen chuckled in sarcasm. "Who?"

It was then that someone else walked into the room. As the figure shut the door behind him, he looked into the smiling face and felt his mouth drop.

"Hello Lord Brightblade," said the man.

Kaylen hissed. "Gabriel..."

The knight looked at everyone and stormed out of the room. How dare them! He would not partake in this scheme to try and raise more money from people who did not have it. They were exploiting from the very people who kept West End alive and they cared nothing but the lining of their own pockets. Rurik had been right about Edwin and he was going to do something about it.

Chapter Eight

The next morning was bright and clear with a small chill in the air so Kaylen decided that he needed some alone time in order to think. He saddled his horse and trotted across the hard fields to one of the forests that lined West End. As he rode he tried to clear his mind of his troubles. They would be there when he returned to the manor and were not likely to go away any time soon.

The forest was bare of leaves but the branches of trees still sprouted out at weird and awkward angles. They moved against the small wind like arms reaching out to touch him. He in return would duck and change direction as if to avoid them. His mount made almost no noise as he walked her through the damp ground and on more than one occasion he jumped a deer or two only to watch them prance across the forest floor seeking some sort of shelter.

Kaylen rode for several hours. He crossed the forest, skipped across several brooks, and finally came out on the edge of a small hamlet. There were a half dozen small waddle and thatch homes with perhaps a score of men, women, and children out to enjoy a beautiful winter day. A small stone alter was placed in the center of the hamlet with a crude wood cross placed in the center. As he reined in, half dozen men gathered about him.

"Hello," said Kaylen. He introduced himself and asked if someone here was in charge. An older man, perhaps in his fifties, with ragged clothing approached.

"I am Rangar," said the man.

Kaylen looked about the village. They were the poor of Kesh. Ragged clothing, simple homes, few possessions, and a makeshift pen holding a few pigs and sheep. He didn't know what they did to earn their meager earnings but he knew if they traded in West End any more it would hardly be worth the effort.

"Have you met a large man recently? He would have come from West End?"

"Aye," replied Rangar. "He came a couple weeks ago and told us that the market was raising its prices in order for us to do business there."

"How do you feel about that?"

"With all respect my lord, it is nothing more than a bunch of pig shit." He lowered his head in hopes of not drawing wrath from the knight. And he wouldn't.

"Ignore it," said Kaylen. "My name is Kaylen Brightblade, I am an Etarian Knight and I own my own land in West End. Might I suggest you spread the word to the neighboring villages that if they don't want to pay the high tariffs in West End, that they might consider having their own market at my manor?"

"And your rates my lord?"

Kaylen had to think for about a second before answering. "Pay what you can afford. If you have a good day at the market, just give a little something extra. If you don't, well then we'll have a feast at the end of the day and all drink to our misery."

This brought cheers among the gathered men.

"Why are you doing this my lord?" asked one.

"Because it is unfair to you and your kinsmen. I agree with the original payment that you provided West End and I do thank you for it. But as an Etarian Knight I cannot enforce ridiculous amounts that you do not have. Mind you, this is temporary Rangar. If West End lowers it prices back to the original amount, I expect you to honor it."

"We will my lord," beamed the leader with a smile. "We will indeed and I will spread the word around."

Kaylen smiled and gave a simple nod. He spent the rest of the day and well into the night visiting other small gatherings and told the same story over and over again. Tanners, farmers, and hunters all rejoiced at the sight of the knight and his words. They would not bow down to West End and it's rising of trading prices. Sure, they felt sorry for the village and offered to help repair it if they could, but they would not be taken advantage of if he could help it. He just wished Brulan would give him some help.

God had to be listening because he was awakened by a large beaming smile and foul breath. Kaylen wiped the sleep from his eyes as he threw his feet onto the cold stone floor.

"By God Rurik what are you doing here?" he asked. He quickly went to a partition in the stone and relieved himself of a full bladder and then proceeded to get dressed.

"I've received news from carrier pigeon," said Rurik. "It seems that help is coming from Brulan!"

"What?"

Kaylen took the small message that had been attached to the bird's leg and read it. There wasn't much information as to be expected but it was enough to bring some hope to West End. "At least I don't feel alone in this anymore. Do you know this Lord Markel?"

"I've heard of him," replied Rurik. "I don't know anything about him really other than the fact that he's an able knight with decent holdings throughout Kesh. I hear he's a fair man."

Kaylen's mind began to race. If they left today or tomorrow then they would be here in two weeks, maybe a little longer if the weather turned bad. He felt a new excitement in him as he quickly finished dressing and ran to the door. He had to tell Edwin. With this news surely the man would reconsider overcharging the nearby villages for bringing their trade here.

Kaylen hurried out the gate of Brightblade Manor and strolled down the hill toward the main street of West End. Even though it was winter, a lot of the people had pulled together and made the village a comfortable place to live once again. He crossed the center of town to where Edwin kept once of his places of business, The Red Star Inn. Between him and Willow Guthrie, there was a friendly exchange of business and although his inn was twice as clean and luxurious he made his real money when high paying travelers coasted through during the summer months.

Edwin's office was located in the back end of the building. The room was expansive, but quite adequately lit. The walls were painted in soft amber, broken up by sheer, springtime green curtains on the windows. The large businessman was seated behind an enormous desk piled with parchment and rolled scrolls. Edwin looked up and gave the knight a somewhat grim smile.

"If it isn't the prodigal knight," said the businessman sarcastically.

Kaylen flinched. He wasn't prepared for this at all. In fact he had come with the good news that a detachment of soldiers were coming to aide in the defenses of the village. "I'm sorry that if my presence bothers you Edwin."

"Do you know why I am such a good businessman Kaylen?" asked Edwin. "I'll tell you. It's because I have the tendency to keep abreast of what is going on around my town. Take this for example, last night I had a man from an outlying hamlet come into town. He got drunk in my inn and started spilling some nasty story about how he and all his friends were going to take their goods to Brightblade Manor for market. He was yelling that West End was full of money grubbers and this new knight of the manor was going to set things right." He leaned back and crossed his hands across his large stomach. "So tell me Lord Brightblade, is this true?"

Kaylen felt his stomach tighten. "Y-yes it is Edwin. I thought it was necessary to send you and the others a message."

"Really? What message would that be?"

"That you can't line your pockets and raise prices like this without thinking of the people and their situation."

Edwin shot forward. "Don't tell me I'm not thinking of West End boy! Why do you think we decided on raising prices? Our people have been through a great travesty and are receiving little to no help from Brulan."

"The town looks like it's doing okay. The whole population has done marvels over the past few months. Why should we raise our market prices?"

"Because all of that work cost money, which we lost a great deal of when we were raided. Families weren't the only thing destroyed you young fool." Edwin held up a scroll wrapped in a protective sheath. "Do you know what this is? This is a letter addressed to the senate telling them that you are overstepping your bounds regarding position in West End."

Kaylen grew flush. "Overstepping my position? What the hell are you talking about? We had orcs on our doorstep and my men and I took them out. How can you say that I overstepped my bounds?"

"Because although you did that, you had no right to go over the town councils decision to raise market prices. That is neither your duty nor your decision. I don't care if you think you're a noble or not, your duty is merely to protect the town and villages around here from danger, not to run its everyday affairs."

Kaylen moved forward.

Edwin stood up to defend himself but never had the opportunity to do so for a figure emerged from the darkness. Gabriel rushed forward to step in front of the knight.

"Hold it there Lord Brightblade," said Gabriel.

The two men stood toe to toe. Kaylen was taller but the newly appointed sheriff of West End was built more solid. What one lacked in size, the other made up in girth. They eyed each other, each wanting the other to make a move. For Kaylen he held Gabriel as a coward who couldn't handle battle. For Gabriel he resented the knight for being a fatherless brat who managed to get into the rungs of high society.

"What is this?" asked Kaylen.

"Gabriel is sheriff inside West End Kaylen," said Edwin sternly. "Now that you offered to have a market inside your compound some could say that is a bold move to start rioting among the members of this town. I'm sure the leaders in Brulan wouldn't like that."

"I consider it free market trade," countered Kaylen.

"But you are not a businessman young man. I am."

"Maybe I'm expanding my roots."

Kaylen glared at the two men, refusing to back down to them and their ideas of prosperity at the expense of the town's citizens. "Just go back to the way things were Edwin. That's all it will take."

Edwin sighed. "Young man you have a lot to learn about business dealings. Why don't you go back and chase your orcs or whatever around and leave the financial dealings of West End to me?"

"I will," replied Kaylen. "Just as soon as you agree to cut the tariffs back to the original prices. The nearby villages can't afford these prices and you know it." Neither was backing down and Kaylen was growing weary playing these games. "What's it going to be Edwin?"

Edwin sighed. He caught a glimpse of Gabriel fingering the hilt of his sword. He knew Kaylen would cut the man down before he could even clear his weapon. No, violence wasn't in it. This time.

"Fair enough Lord Brightblade," said the businessman. "I will return tariffs to their original prices, but no lower."

Kaylen simply nodded. "Thank you."

He turned and began to leave. As he reached for the door Edwin grunted. "Oh, what was it you wanted?"

The knight turned. "Brulan is sending help. A knight and his men at arms are coming. You made a wise decision Edwin."

Edwin could only sit and clench his fist in anger.

Chapter Nine

Isabella Brightblade liked to think of herself as one who took extra precautions in life. Since her husband refused to talk to her about her step-son and his new position, she took even more protection against what she was about to do. The man she hired was taking his sweet time in getting rid of Kaylen and had not kept her informed on what he was doing. The fact that he was considered one of the best at these sorts of things was starting to wear on her mind if she had been lied to. She decided that things were not going as planned and was prepared to make some extra efforts to foil the bastard son of Augustus. Like any military post, Brulan's officers could barely keep their lips tight whenever alcohol was involved and within a few days word had gotten to her that Lord Markel and his men would be making a stop in West End on their way to Redmere. It really wasn't a stop because West End was further past so immediately she suspected that Augustus had arranged for this to happen. For what reason, she didn't know but she was going to find out.

Isabella walked with a quickened pace. She was in the Senate District where the powerful politicians lived in grand marbled homes with huge pillars supporting red clayed rooftops. Bubbling fountains set among freshly trimmed flower gardens gave off a serene atmosphere that showed little of the behind the scenes working of the continent's most powerful government. The Senate House was set at the end of a long road with beautiful shops that catered to the high paid officials and their families. It was a massive structure with grand pillars and archways separated by more statues, gardens, and walkways that kept out anyone who didn't work or belong there. She gave a smug grin as she walked one of those paths. This was where she should have been, here with someone who tasted real power, not the wife of an army officer who had outlived his usefulness.

Isabella went to the rear of the building where a single man sat alone at a small pool. His face was transfixed to the water where a dozen fish swam in circles as he tossed bits of bread to them. As she approached he turned.

"Lady Brightblade," he said without a smile.

"Senator Kinesh," she replied with a firm lip.

They had known each other for many years. Despite that, one could hardly call them friends. Each had their own ideas of power, one on the society level the other in the political spectrum. Senator Kinesh was the majority leader of the Kesh Business Movement, a consortium of business and guild leaders set to increase revenue among the higher noble houses in the country.

"You're man is taking his sweet time," she commented as she edged around the pool. "Makes me wonder if my money was well spent."

"It was I assure you," he replied. "The reason Atticus is so good is that he takes his time and thinks things through, unlike a common killer."

"Well he's taking way too long in my opinion. I've heard through my own sources that Lord Markel is making a stop in West End. Why is that?"

Kinesh shrugged his bony shoulders. "I don't know. I'm a politician not a member of the elite military like your husband."

"Don't patronize me senator. I want Markel stopped before he reaches West End."

"Good grief woman why? So what if the army shows up in West End? What is it to you?"

Isabella fumed. "Because I want West End to fall! If Kaylen somehow manages to survive your assassin then he'll keep control of the manor and of the town."

Kinesh shook his head. "This isn't a feudal system we live in Lady Brightblade. This is a democracy. Your step-son does not control the village, he merely protects it."

"He isn't my step-son!" she spat angrily.

Kinesh couldn't help but smile. "My dear lady you may not like it, but Kaylen Brightblade is your husband's son. Therefore, he is your step-son. He has a legitimate claim to do your husband's bidding. Maybe you need to take it up with Augustus."

"But Augustus is the one who appointed him lord of the manor!"

"-and according to law, he has that right."

Isabella spun around in anger. This was getting out of hand! She had to do something, but what? She thought for a few moments before turning back around. "So who is the mayor of West End now?"

Kinesh eyed her carefully, wondering what was going through her head and what she was going to expect of him. He had enough troubles in the senate without playing mind games with this pompous woman. "Edwin Deplato is the man who is the acting representative there. He's a businessman by nature."

"Is he part of your organization?"

He waited but finally nodded his head. "Yes. He's an acting member of the KBM. Why?"

"Because I want to talk to him that's why. As part of the KBM he should have an interest in what is going on in West End, don't you think?"

Kinesh could only nod.

"Good. Then you need to contact him and have him give Kaylen a hard time. That young brat won't know what to do with the political side of his position and I'm sure that he'll resign the manor back to his father."

Kinesh arched an eyebrow. "So you want me to use my powers to torment Kaylen? Is that what you're asking me to do?"

Isabella narrowed her eyes. "That is precisely what I'm asking you to do. Whether it is from your assassin or the political shrewdness you have I want to drive that boy from one of my homes."

The politician gave her a sly look. "You are a pretentious bitch, aren't you Lady Brightblade?"

Isabella scowled back with a lowered lip. "You have no idea."

Darkness was the one friend Atticus Bane counted on. He felt more at ease after the sun went down so he could glide in and out of the streets and back alleys of a major city. However, even though he felt at home, he did feel a little vulnerable in the open confines of the fields surrounding West End. Once he arrived on the outskirts, he stopped for a few moments behind a shed to get his bearing. To his left loomed Brightblade Manor, a small fortress by most standards, but still one to be reckoned with. His contact inside the town told him he would have no problem entering and that with a man of his skill, his task would be over before anyone knew anything about it.

Atticus took a deep breath. He took a step toward the hill where the manor stood over the town. Moving with extreme care and quietness to avoid detection, he moved with the stealth of a cat seeking its prey. He walked along the shadows, seeking the small but barren trees for every little bit of protection they could muster.

Off in the distance he heard a dog bark in the town below. He froze in his tracks near some bushes. He looked in the direction of the noise and discovered the mutt was barking at a pair of drunks stumbling home after a night of drinking. He mentally cursed them and began to make his way back up the hill.

Reaching the top, Atticus did a quick glance and found a lone sentry standing at the top of the wall, his arms folded across his chest, head lowered. Stupid bastard, thought Atticus. He crept around the side and away from the sleeping guard. He circled the wall slowly, his keen eyes looking for some sort of advantage. Atticus was good and he had done this many times before. It only took a few minutes for him to find what he was looking for. A thin vine hung loosely by roots that had snaked their way into the small cracks of the stones that made up the structure. Atticus smiled.

He tugged on it a few times and was surprised that it held his weight. His luck was holding and he intended to use its full advantage in succeeding. Wrapping his gloved hands around the vine he pulled himself up.

Years of living the life as an assassin had made Atticus very nimble. He used the vine to pull his body weight then jab his boot into whatever small pocket of space he could find. With each step upward his muscles ached at the constant climbing motion. Finally he reached the top and slid over to the cold hard walkway. He lay there for several moments catching his breath and keeping a keen ear open to any sounds from anyone out in the cold night air. Once he was satisfied that no one was out, Atticus continued on.

The assassin moved along the ramparts with ease. He knew little about the castle with the exception that the men at arms numbered around a dozen and with the servants and other minor workers, perhaps twenty people total lived in the structure. He kept to the dark as he made his way to the courtyard in silence. Atticus stopped in the yard and took refuge behind a wagon filled with straw. He took a few minutes to get his bearing and then raced to the twin doors leading to the hall.

The hall was simple with a long table and chairs along with a fireplace off to the far wall. Embers from the evening fire were still glowing and giving off a fair amount of heat into the room. Atticus noticed a set of spiraled stairs off in an adjoining room. He removed one of his short swords from the scabbards across his back. With the grace of a cat he made his way up the stairs.

Atticus remembered the conversation he had with his agent in West End. This corridor had doors on both sides of the hall that served as the small simple quarters of the men at arms. At the end of the hall was another set of stairs that led upward. It was here that his target lay.

A large oak door was shut before him. Atticus tried the knob. Just as he thought, the door was locked so he would have to resort to the one thing he hated. Laying his weapon aside he reached into the dark fold of his clothing and removed a small pouch with some tools. He took the tiny instruments and began working the lock. Atticus took his time for he didn't want to give his opponent any chance of discovering him. Gradually he worked the tumblers back and forth before he heard a barely audible click. With a grim smile he replaced the tools with his sword.

Atticus took a careful look around. Everyone was still in sleep. He was lucky that this was working out so well. He hadn't remembered when the gods of old had been so generous to him. He said a silent prayer to no god in particular and eased the door open.

The room was like the rest of the castle, quaint and small. On the opposite side of the room, a figure could be seen huddled underneath the simple gray wool blanket. He moved forward. He stepped up to the bed and then realized he had made a mistake.

"It seems as though my luck has just run out," he muttered.

Kaylen Brightblade emerged from a dark corner. In his hands he held a crossbow the iron tipped bolt aimed directly to the back of Atticus's head. "I don't know who you are mister but I would think very carefully about what you're about to do."

"It appears I'm about to do nothing since you're standing behind me. I'm not a fool. I know you have some sort of weapon out ready to use against me."

"And why shouldn't I? You're nothing but a robber coming to either take from me or hold me for ransom. Whichever it is my friend you will not get much for my retched soul."

"May I turn around?" asked Atticus.

"Might as well face the man who's about to kill you."

Atticus turned around. His sword was hanging in his hand but he saw no opportunity of it. He took in the young man standing before him. He was tall with tight muscles pressing against his clothing. "My name is Atticus Bane. I was sent here to kill you."

"A hired killer? Let me guess, Edwin Delapost hired you to get rid of me, is that correct?"

Atticus chuckled. "You know I can't tell you that. An assassin might not have much but the one thing they will or should not do is name their employer. So perhaps young Kaylen Brightblade we can just ignore your question for right now."

Kaylen gestured with his weapon. "I think I should shoot you right now and just be done with it."

"You could," agreed Atticus. "But you won't do it will you Lord Brightblade."

Kaylen shrugged. "I really haven't decided it yet really." He motioned to the window against the wall. "So are you the one to blame for the mess in our town?"

"You mean the raiders who attacked your town? That wasn't me my friend. Whoever did that is long gone from here now."

"How do you know that?"

"Because they were nothing more than mere bandits who wanted one last raid before winter set in. Believe me son they are long gone."

Atticus waited anxiously. He saw something in the young man's eyes but wasn't quite sure what it was. Hesitation perhaps? It wasn't fear. "So what do we do now Brightblade?"

"I haven't decided yet," replied Kaylen in a cool voice. For some unknown reason he backed away a little causing the hairs on the back of Atticus' neck to rise a little. "Like I said maybe I'll just kill you and be done with it. That would send a message to your employer that he wasted his gold."

Atticus shrugged. "You could do that but then you would just have a larger bounty on your head. Once word got out you'd have more than just me to deal with."

"Then I'll take your kind out one at a time until the contract is lifted or I run out of bodies."

Atticus tilted his head. "Well look what we have here. A knight without a consciousness about him. You would really leave bodies littered about the land. Word would spread that you were a wild knight without proper discipline."

"I'm a knight not of choice but of convenience. Much like everything in my life."

The assassin took in the words. In a sad sort of way he felt sorry for the young man. He was nothing more than a pawn in a game of high ranking nobles in Brulan. He shouldn't have cared but maybe it was his age slowly creeping up on him because he actually felt something for this young man. Of course, he was holding a crossbow with a very painful looking bolt pointed in his direction.

"You and I have something in common then," Atticus told Kaylen. "For that I think I will spare you for the time being."

Kaylen laughed. "You forget assassin that I am the one holding the weapon aimed at your despicable face."

Atticus grinned. Then, everything went into fast motion. The assassin moved, slightly but enough to cause the young knight to flinch. With his sword arm Atticus swung his weapon upwards. There was a crack as the sharp blade cut into the crossbow. Kaylen panicked and pulled the lever causing the weapon to discharge. The iron bolt flew thru the air and smacked harmlessly against a stone wall. In one fluid motion Atticus turned and swept his leg out toward his opponent. Kaylen crashed to the floor with a loud thump and then the assassin was upon him.

Atticus kicked him in the side and followed thru with another kick to the young man's stomach. Kaylen moaned in pain but the assassin ignored the sound and pinned him to the ground. Placing the point of his sword against the knight's throat Atticus once again looked into Kaylen's eyes.

"You aren't scared are you?" he asked.

"N-no," replied the knight.

"Why?"

"Because like you I am an abomination to society. But unlike you I do have some sort of honor about me and however I got here I know in my heart that God will welcome me because I was fair and protected this town with the best of my ability."

Atticus sneered. "You are so sure of yourself."

The assassin flicked his wrist and a small cut appeared on Kaylen's throat. It wasn't deadly but it would leave a mark for a while. As blood trickled to the floor Atticus noted pain on the young man's face, but still his eyes bore no fear. For some reason Atticus jumped to his feet and kicked the young man away. With several strides he was at the only window in the room. He jumped on the sill and looked into the darkness. He was glad he was alive and for some strange reason glad that he did not kill the young man. He turned back and looked at the knight struggling to his feet. Atticus pointed his sword at Kaylen.

"Remember this Lord Brightblade," he hissed. "When you have the opportunity to kill your opponent you should take the advantage. That is my advice to you. I let you live tonight so that you may know two things. One is to let you know you are a marked man. Someone is trying to kill you, so remember that. The second thing is that a bad storm is coming your way and how you handle it will determine what kind of knight you really are."

Kaylen gasped for air as he got to his feet. "But why? Why didn't you kill me now and collect your bounty."

Atticus smiled. "I don't know. Maybe because I sense something in you. Something worthy that I haven't had in a long while. We will meet again Lord Brightblade, of that I am sure. Perhaps then we will see who is the greater of us. Or then again, perhaps we will see who is darker and much worse."

With that said, Atticus Bane jumped into the night.

Chapter Ten

"Why you let go?" asked the orc chieftain.

"Seemed like the right thing to do," replied Atticus. He sat around a campfire in the early morning smoking his pipe weed and drinking a hot cup of herbal tea, one of his favorites.

"You no good for clan," said Vokar. "Ruddock clan will take care of problem. You no longer welcome assassin."

The large figure started to leave but Atticus whistled. "I told you that I could give him to you. We agreed on nothing about me killing him. In fact, unless you agree to pay me for a contract I think I'll let him live."

"I no need you human. You think about that. I nor Ruddock clans do not need you."

"Fine," said Atticus taking a sip of tea. "I will just leave and you can deal with this knight on your own."

"You should kill him. You had chance. Maybe you scared?"

Atticus snickered. "That will be the day," he told the orc. "Maybe I will just move on. You obviously know where you're going and how to get into the manor."

Vokar growled. "Watch tongue human. I no patience for you to joke."

"Suit yourself," said Atticus. "I'll be leaving after I get a few hours rest."

The assassin managed to get a couple hours sleep before he was awakened by the chieftain. Vokar had second thoughts and asked once again if Atticus would help. The latter was reluctant in a way but then gold was laid out before him and he no reason not to play along. He agreed but told him that they would have to wait three days before doing anything. When asked why Atticus just said that he needed time to prepare for the battle as well as they all should.

So while the orc chieftain prepared his troops, Atticus headed back toward West End. It was a dangerous thing to do he knew but he had an asset in town, someone who could provide him with the information he needed. Vokar started to object but as Atticus explained; if the orcs wanted to win the battle then he needed to go.

The trip back to West End was slow going. As usual he took different routes instead of a direct one which made the trip longer. However he used this time to reflect on the events folding out before him. One of his greatest attributes was to be able to turn forces against each other and keep his name out of the equation. Oh sure, he had killed before, many times in fact. Still, he didn't like to advertise the fact of his career although the name was well known throughout the land.

Atticus didn't normally care but for some reason this time was a little different. Something else was going on here. He had been involved in power plays between political or military factions before but this time it was between a family. Perhaps he shouldn't have cared since he did this for profit but in a way he felt something for the young Kaylen Brightblade. He wasn't a bad person from what he had found out. The nearby villagers had no problem with the lord that protected them from the orcs or bandits when they ran through the area. He held contempt for his employer. She cared nothing except for social status and it was apparent to him that Kaylen was a thorn in her side. But to put out a death bounty on him? That was harsh. He suspected there was more going on behind the scenes with Lady Isabella but unless it involved him directly he was going to stay out of it. He would fulfill his contract but when and how he did it was still in question. Could the orcs take out the West End defenders? It was possible even though they weren't the brightest creatures in the world. The one thing they did have going for them were the numbers. If nothing else, they would overwhelm West End and tear it to the ground.

Then there was something else. For some reason the encounter with Kaylen brought forth exhilaration. That was something that he hadn't felt in some time. His previous targets were the rouge politicians, generals, or cheating businessmen. He could care less and most times it had been quick and silent. But now, with the young knight it brought back old feelings of his youth when he had gone toe to toe in battle. Oh what a feeling that had been!

Atticus spurred his horse a little harder. He wanted to get to West End and see his contact. If he was going to carry this out he wanted to know everything as soon as possible. By the end of the day he would be there and he would begin to start the game.

"You should have killed him Kaylen," said Darius. "By God man you wasted a perfect opportunity."

"Lay off him will you?" snapped Lars.

Darius shook his head and went to the table to refresh his wine. When he was out of earshot Lars leaned down to Kaylen's chair. "He's right you know milord. It would have been easier to do."

"I thought about believe me," said Kaylen. "Ouch!"

Riva looked up from bandaging his ribs. "Sorry. Well, not really you fool. I agree with them you should have killed him."

"I know," was all Kaylen could say. He shook his head in disgust. They were right. He had the assassin right where he wanted him and he was hesitant to pull the trigger. For his leniency he had gotten a couple cracked ribs and the ever present threat that Atticus Bane would return.

"So what now?" asked Lars.

Kaylen was about to answer when the door of the hall snapped open. They all flinched at the cold and flames sputtered in the fireplace. Bishop Rurik Ironside strolled in with a waddle, his little dwarf legs pounding across the stone floor.

"Blasted fool," snorted Rurik. He made the sign of the cross and slapped the young knight across the back. "Should've killed the bastard right then and there."

"I know," replied with exhaustion.

The patrons in the room chuckled and Darius brought the cleric a tankard of ale. So they all sat around the fire as Riva continued her work. Kaylen noticed her golden hair shine in the firelight. He felt his head stir but then took his eyes away as she looked at him.

"Father?" asked Kaylen.

Rurik shook his head. "I don't know yet. Winter is fast approaching so I'm hoping the assassin left for the time being."

"What about the orcs? Think they'll come anymore this winter?"

"I doubt it," replied the dwarf. He took a healthy swig from his tankard and let out a large belch. "The orcs will probably stay in the northern area of the mountains. They'll return in spring I'm sure but for the time being I think we're safe."

The three warriors all nodded, each relieved in some extent. They were cold, tired, and ready to repair their equipment during the next few months. Each man would be allowed a week's leave during this time in order to take care of personal business though most of that meant drinking.

"How long until the detachment gets here?" asked Lars.

"I'm hoping within the next week or so at the latest. Once they arrive I will let you all either stay or go. I know you have more important things to do than watch my home and chase orcs and bandits."

"We're staying on," replied Darius. "All of us, right Rurik?"

"That's right," said Rurik. "Your men love you and all want to stay if you will allow."

"I can barely pay you all," said Kaylen.

Lars stood and went to the fire to warm his hands. He then turned back to the group. "I have sufficient income for now."

"Well I don't," commented Darius, "but I will stay as well to keep your asses out of trouble."

They sat there for the majority of the day going over the reports and what they knew was going on. Clouds were on the horizon and Rurik said he had a feeling that a storm would be here within a few days.

"What will happen when the new detachment gets here," asked Lars. "Do we just return to the town and our lives?"

"What do you mean?" asked Rurik. "You're the security of the town. That doesn't change just because Lord Markel is coming. As far as the laws of Kesh go, as well as the wishes of Augustus, Kaylen is lord of the keep. You will keep your position Lars don't worry."

"Bishop Ironside you just said we are the protectors of the town. If that is true then why is Delapost honoring Gabriel as sheriff?"

"Aye," replied the priest. He rubbed his grizzly beard. "I see your point. I am of the priesthood, not a politician thank God. However, I must confess that I should clear my speaking. Delapost is the mayor of West End and with the council appointing Gabriel as sheriff we must follow the law. They are the leaders inside the town. However, Brightblade Manor sits outside the towns boundaries, if only by a few hundred yards. Technically speaking, they can play their game inside the boundaries of West End. However, you all are the protectors of the lands surrounding the town." He shook his head and slammed a meaty fist into the palm of his other hand. "Blasted laws and politics! Sometimes they get so confusing."

They all chuckled at his frustration though it wasn't a laughing matter.

"So what do we do?" asked Darius.

Everyone looked toward Kaylen. The young man stared ahead, his mind focusing on a million things at one time.

"We protect the lands," he finally said. "As of right now that is all we can do."

Chapter Eleven

Atticus came from the shadows. He tossed his overcoat onto the back of the chair. A thin narrowed face looked up from across the table.

"Well?" he asked.

The figure shrugged. "What is it you want to know?"

"I want to know about this knight of yours. I know very little and it is hard for me to do my job if you can't provide me with information."

"He's a young man," came the reply.

"No shit," said Atticus with distaste. "Don't fuck around with me. I'm not in the mood for it. It's cold out there and I haven't been offered a drink."

A steaming cup of gray liquid was placed before him. The assassin took a drink. It was rather bitter but warm enough to chill his cold bones. "I'm not going to ask what this is."

"Probably better you don't," said the figure.

Atticus sat there for several minutes letting the warm liquor work through his body. When he felt comfortable enough he reached into his folds and produced his pipe. He ignited the smoke weed with a flint and took a heavy drag.

"Atticus is a strange young man," said the figure. "He came here several years ago and was placed in the castle on the hill by Augustus Brightblade. Few people know of his past, even I don't know. It is rumored that he is a son of the old knight but for some reason Lady Isabella doesn't claim him."

They don't know he's a bastard, thought Atticus. Oh well, weren't they all at some point? "Go on," he said.

"After the attack on West End by the bandits Augustus appointed him lord of the manor. He gathered in a few poor souls to serve as men at arms, perhaps a dozen. A few left though after they attacked an orc raiding party."

"Orcs?" asked Atticus. "This far from the mountains at this time of the year?"

"So it seems," came the reply. "Then again they are stupid creatures for the most point I think. I hear our boys killed them on, the young Kaylen taking care of three of them personally. Probably the first time he's taken a life of any sort."

"How does he lead?"

The figure shrugged again. "Don't really know. Like I said three of the men left the manor and returned here. Next thing I know they are made sheriff and guards to keep the town safe."

"Thought that was Brightblade's job?"

There was a chuckle. "Right. Kesh laws forbid Etarian Knights to enter a town and evoke law unless it is approved by the senate or requested by the mayor of said town. Neither has occurred here."

"What about the other villages nearby? Do they know about this young knight?"

"Of course," replied the figure with a slight smile. "In fact they sort of love the young man."

"How so?"

There was a long sigh. "It seems as though Edwin Delapost, he's the mayor here right now, sent word that tariffs would increase when the trade season started. Of course the outlying villages hated that. Young Brightblade went and offered to have the patrons of these villagers trade at his manor. His estate is outside the town boundaries of course so there would be little if any tariffs imposed by him."

"Thus winning the support of the outlying areas while hampering with the progress of West End."

There was a nod this time from the figure. "Yes. Half the town is mad at him while half are glad because they didn't really want the tariff increase anyway. Some individuals fear the nearby villages will go to Redmere to do their trading."

"Another day away at the least."

"At least, probably more if they use wagons. But a bigger audience to sell to for sure."

Atticus thought about this for a little bit. He then inched closer to his agent. "Would this be considered an act of treason against a settlement of Kesh? Damaging trade, cutting out the town of progress from someone who is supposed to be protecting them?"

"Maybe. But it worked though because Delapost agreed to keep the tariffs the original cost. Brightblade played an aggressive move and it worked. Now everything is back to normal for the time being. Good thing too. Word has it a contingent is coming from Brulan to check on young Brightblade." The figure chuckled. "With a hundred new men in the village our profits will be okay we hope. In fact we're counting on it."

Atticus arched an eyebrow. "When will this contingent be here?"

"Week, maybe more. Snow is coming in I fear so it could take a little longer."

Damn, thought Atticus. Another knight bringing his troops to West End wasn't an appealing thought. His orc buddies would be hard pressed to take the town with an experienced knight and troops here.

"Anything else?" asked Atticus.

The figure seemed to think a moment. "No not really. Personally I think Kaylen Brightblade is doing a fine job. Of course he is young and hasn't really dealt with anything major. Time will tell."

"So you like him?"

There was another shrug of the shoulders. "He is likeable. Personally I have nothing against him. He hasn't hurt me or my business."

Atticus shoved a gold coin across the table. "For your troubles."

The stranger pocketed the coin and moved away leaving Atticus to his own lonely thoughts.

Chapter Twelve

Kaylen had just finished breakfast when word came from one of the sentries at the main gate. A visitor had come to Brightblade Manor asking to speak to the lord. Kaylen took a look outside the hall. The sky was gray and a medium wind blew from the north giving quite a chill to the air. He looked across the small courtyard and was surprised to see Edwin Delapost all wrapped up in a heavy cloak. What in the world could this man possibly want?

"Allow him to come in," he said.

Kaylen turned around and saw Riva clearing away the dishes from breakfast. "Can you bring some more hot tea and another cup?"

Riva curtsied and gave him a warm smile. He had told her not to do that but she insisted he was a lord now and etiquette required it. Still, with the growing feelings he was having for her it felt wrong and out of place.

Kaylen took up his seat at the table and took a sip of the remaining of the tea. It was good and warm in the pit of his stomach, much as the sausage, cheese, and bread had been for breakfast. Riva came in poured him some more and set the warm jug and another pitcher on the table. As she ran back to the kitchen he caught himself watching her backside.

As did someone else.

"Ah is love in the air?" asked a smiling Edwin as he bounced forward.

Kaylen turned, his face growing stern. "May I help you Edwin?"

"By the looks of everything it seems that you've already been helped."

The knight narrowed his eyes. "Careful of your words Edwin. You are in Brightblade Manor now, not the confines of your town with your cowardly sheriff."

"Gabriel? Cowardly? I hardly think so. He's kept the town safe from the drunkards and thieves that sometimes frequent here."

"Drunks are not what West End needs to be afraid of and you know it. Orcs are out there."

"Ah," replied Edwin. "You say that, but I haven't seen one of those green skinned bastards around here in some time."

"Mark my word they'll come sooner or later."

"Well," said Edwin, "I think you're just making all this to be more than it is. Orcs haven't come around these parts. Maybe the outlying villages from time to time, but not West End."

Kaylen sighed. There was no use pleading his case to this man. It would be a waste of time and energy and after the attack with the assassin he didn't have the energy to argue. "What can I do for you Edwin?" he finally asked. He waved to a seat across the table and the man sat down with a thump. Kaylen offered him the hot tea which Edwin took greedily.

"Not bad," he said after taking a sip.

"Edwin. Please," stated Kaylen.

The businessman cleared his throat. "Yes. The reason I'm here. I hear you were attacked the other night by an assassin. Are you okay?"

Kaylen eyed him suspiciously. "Yes I'm fine."

"Any ideas on who would want to kill you?"

"Other than you, the village council, and Gabriel? Not really. But the three I named are my prime suspects."

Edwin snorted at the thought. "We may have disagreements with you Lord Brightblade but even to plan an act of murder towards an Etarian Knight would be treason. I can't believe you would even consider that notion."

"And I can't believe this man broke into my castle, past my sentry, and tried to kill me."

"I'm as shocked as you milord. I assure you neither I nor the council would even dare."

"Gabriel?"

"Tsk. He can handle the drunks and thieves milord but he doesn't have the skills to commit murder or even hire someone to do it. There has to be someone else."

Kaylen kept his suspicions. The things Edwin was saying made sense in a way but he wasn't the one who was attacked. If the portly man was right, then who would want him dead? They had killed the orcs and he seriously doubted they would send an assassin to take him out. They were too proud and powerful to do that. Plus, they fought among themselves just as much as humans. But who?

"I've come to offer a truce," said Edwin. "West End cannot afford to have its council and its lord protector fighting among themselves."

Kaylen folded his arms across his chest. "I didn't start this Edwin. You did with that ridiculous tariff barrier."

Edwin gave a slight shrug. "Perhaps. I had the best interest of West End at heart."

Kaylen relaxed some. He reached out for his tea, his mind in thought. "Perhaps you did Edwin," he said after taking a drink. "Perhaps you really do care about the whole future of our village and want to see it succeed and grow. I have no problems with that. But, if that were to happen it's going to have to happen with the help of the smaller villages and hamlets. Their trade with us is important right now and we can't go off raising taxes so much. I know we need the money, I know that I also owe you much for your assistance in paying for the men at arms."

Kaylen realized something. "It wouldn't be you to order me dead. I owe you money for helping in paying for men. You would lose money if I were to die."

Edwin smiled. "Precisely boy. That is why I came here to talk to you. I have no reason to kill you, nor does the council. Without someone in Brightblade Manor to protect us from the wild lands we would easily be overrun. It's happened, you saw it. Now you're appointed to do that job. No Kaylen, we don't want you dead."

The businessman stood to leave. "I must go now. Now that it's settled that we aren't trying to kill you, maybe you can work on finding out who does."

He had hoped to make a quick getaway into the wilderness but like everything else it was unavoidable. Kaylen finished the straps on his boots when the door to his quarters burst open.

"Are you mad?" asked Rurik in a loud voice.

"More like crazy!" spat Darius.

Kaylen looked past them to the third figure walking through the door. "Lars?"

The big man shrugged. "What do you want me to say that hasn't already been said?"

"I don't expect you all to understand," replied Kaylen. "So it has to be this way until I can find out who tried to murder me."

"You have no clues about anything," said Rurik. "So why even go? Maybe this assassin will try again here and then we can nab him. We'll sleep in your quarters with you from now on."

Kaylen shook his head. "No Bishop Ironside. Not this time."

"Bishop? Since when are 'ye so formal with me? Now I know your blooming' mad."

Kaylen couldn't help but smile. "Stop it. I'll be fine I promise."

"Then let one of us go with you at least," said Darius.

"Nor you or Lars either my friend. This is something I have to do and you know it. I can't have an assassin showing up here. You all know that. We have enough to worry about as it is. You all still have duties to perform here, I expect that."

They all three mumbled something but Kaylen ignored the comments. Deep down inside they knew this was probably for the best but they had become friends and when men shared that bond it was hard to see one put into danger.

"You know it's going to snow the next few weeks," said Rurik.

"What better time to track an assassin?" commented Kaylen with a grin. "He'll never expect it." With that said, Kaylen strapped on his sword belt and put his heavy cloak over his shoulders. He started for the door when Lars reached and touched his arm. They locked eyes. Kaylen could see a tint of moisture in his friend's eyes.

"Not you too," he whispered to Lars.

"Be careful and come back to us," was the only thing that the man could say.

"I will. I promise."

"Where are you going?" asked Rurik.

"To the wilderness. I'm going back to the site where we took the orcs down and move north."

"What makes you think this assassin will be there?"

Kaylen shook his head. "I really don't know. Just a gut feeling. Maybe it's God leading me there Rurik. Maybe that's where my destiny really lies."

"Bah! You're just making that up."

"It's what I feel and I believe that I'll have to go on that if nothing else for the time being."

They said their goodbyes and Kaylen walked out.

Riva stood in the courtyard with the knight's horse. His saddlebags were stocked and his light pack strapped down as well. They looked at each other, neither knowing what to say. Then, without hesitation, Kaylen leaned in and gave her a quick kiss. Her lips were soft and tender. He felt trembling in her skin and as he pulled away a tear slid down her cheek. Without saying a word he slid into his saddle and rode out the gate of Brightblade Manor.

He pushed the white mare hard for the first hour, letting her warm her body in the chilly air. Then, right at noon he slowed her to a walk. He didn't want her wearing down because he had a lot of ground to cover before nightfall.

Around mid-afternoon the first traces of snow began to fall. He pulled his hood up and kept his eyes forward, always scanning the horizon. His mind wandered near and far about the events over the past few days. He had been in a fight with an assassin, made up with Edwin, and now was out on the road looking for the man who tried to kill him. It was a strange world, he thought. He also played in his mind all the possibilities of who would want to kill him. In the back of his mind he kept the words of Edwin fresh and tried to make himself reason that the speech was real. He felt the so called mayor was right in the fact that he had no reason to kill him for the debt that he carried. He really had no enemies here other than the squabble with the council and that really wasn't serious enough to kill over, at least he hoped not.

Kaylen rode past Crooked Shallow. The burned homes were nothing more than skeletons left to rot in the elements. Not a sound came from the village. He made the sign of the cross and prayed to God that he welcomed them into heaven. He shook his head and wondered why the Heavenly Father would allow this. But God had his reasons, he figured. Just like God had his reasons that Kaylen be born fatherless. It had kind of a sinister sounding name to it, he reasoned. The Bastard Knight. A man caught between nobility and the destitute.

As night fell Kaylen stopped at the sign of the attack. There was little more than scraps and a few bones of the attack. Either the creatures of the forests or other orcs had picked the bodies clean. He had heard orcs ate their own but had never witnessed it. He didn't really care one way or the other. It was un-Christian of him he knew, but he hoped their race would someday disappear from the world of Aerola.

Kaylen hobbled his horse and built a quick fire. He knew it was dangerous but it could also be dangerous not to have one. The fire would provide warmth and keep animals away. Then he sat down and as he stared at the flames he let his guard down and enjoyed a meal of salted pork, cheese, and bread. He washed it all down with watered down wine. Afterwards he reached into a pack and withdrew a pipe. He didn't do it very often and without his friends around, he could enjoy the smoke weed without the joking harassment from his friends. Next he pulled out a worn manuscript that Rurik had given him years before. It was a book on the rules and teachings of God. Sometimes he would get confused as the manuscript told of both a stern and a loving God. He felt it should be one way or the other. Only when he could master what the Lord was saying Rurik told him, then he could move on too other teachings as well. But until then, this was the only book he could read. So he settled in for the night, the first night on his own in a long time. It wasn't until he drifted off to sleep that he realized how lonely he really felt.

Chapter Thirteen

"Who that?" asked Vokar.

"That, my orc friend," said Atticus "is the young knight I was telling you about."

A small growl came from the orc. "We must prepare. His men are close."

Atticus shook his head. "He's by himself Vokar."

"Why? He either brave or dumb."

"I'd say he's brave and dumb. But let me handle this."

Vokar growled again. "You kill him now assassin."

"In due time. There's something about him I like and I want to see exactly how strong willed this man is."

"Maybe he knows something."

"That's what I'm going to find out."

Atticus was growing weary of his decision to join up with this rag tag group. If he had the time he would slit all their throats and be done with it. When the time was right he would let the orc have his fun with West End and take the village apart at his whim. Right now he was more interested in the man whom he was paid to kill. For some unknown reason Kaylen Brightblade intrigued him.

With a few gentle leaps and bounds, Atticus jumped from the rocks and onto the snowy ground several yards from Kaylen's horse.

"By God!" swore the knight.

Both men drew their swords and looked at each other. Atticus was impressed that the knight held his horse in check at his sudden presence.

"I told you we would meet again Kaylen," said Atticus with a sneer.

"I'm going to kill you right here and right now like I should have done the night you came into my home."

"Ah yes. Well I'll stand right here while you attack me. I'm a little older so it shouldn't be too hard of a task for you."

Atticus saw the anger in the young man's eyes. He waited and was not disappointed as Kaylen jumped from his saddle and ran toward him. The knight's sword was raised and even in the cloudy morning Atticus could see the blade held a fine edge.

Just as Kaylen reached him he swung with all his might. Stupid boy, thought Atticus. Atticus moved slightly allowing the momentum of Kaylen's strike to carry him past. As a sarcastic move Atticus tapped the boy on the rear with the flat of his sword.

"Watch yourself now," said Atticus with ridicule.

Kaylen regained his composure and swung again. This time Atticus met his attack with his twin short swords causing their meeting to echo in the air.

"Your problem Kaylen is that you are taking this too personally."

The knight swung again and once again the assassin parried the blow. "How else should I take it? You're trying to kill me."

"On the contrary you are the one who jumped from your horse with your sword out ready to chop my head off. I simply wanted to talk to you."

"Liar!"

The swords clashed again. The pair moved around in the snow, their feet trying to gain traction on the slippery ground. Kaylen kept up the attack with such ferocity that Atticus was generally impressed. His initial feeling that the knight could be a worthy opponent was true. For several minutes they squared off but it was only Kaylen that was on the offensive. It took him several moments but the knight soon realized this. He moved back out of range of the assassin's reach.

"Why-are-you toying with me?" asked Kaylen through panted breaths.

"Like I told you Kaylen I just wanted to talk to you."

"Bullshit!"

Atticus shook his head. "You really need to work on your discipline. Do you know that?"

"What?"

"Your discipline Kaylen. It's really bad. You could easily kill me I think, well maybe not easily." He chuckled at his own joke. "Regardless I think you could be really worthy one day."

Kaylen's nostrils flared. He raised the sword again but it never found its mark. A large club came from nowhere and slammed into the back of his head and he went down before the assassin's feet.

"Talk too much," said Vokar.

Stupid beast, thought Atticus. He really hoped the green brute hadn't killed the young man. He never had the opportunity to really taunt someone before he killed them until now. Just as he was having his fun the orc leader had to come in and ruin it.

Several orcs came and gathered up the limp body of the knight and everyone made their way up a rocky slope where the forest began. It leveled out and they entered the new camp that had been set up several days before. The knight was taken to a tree and thrown to the ground without any regard. Shackles were placed on his legs and hands, and then one of the guards kicked him for good measure.

Atticus swore. These beasts had neither honor nor shame. He turned to Vokar who was heading for his hide tent. "What in the Nine Hells are you doing Vokar? I told you I wanted to talk to him."

The big orc spun around. "You not in control. I in control."

"I never said I was in control," said Atticus. "I simply wanted to talk to him is all and now you nearly killed him."

"Time for talk over. We attack now."

Atticus shook his head. "Not a wise idea Vokar."

"Why not?"

"Because you all don't know the layout of the village like I do. There could be an army out there hidden among the buildings or in the hills surrounding it. You'd be cut down. That's why I wanted to talk to him."

"Vokar clan will kill everything. You had chance. Now we do it my way."

"Suit yourself dumbass," cursed Atticus.

There was a roar and the orc reached for his massive sword strapped across his back. Atticus had pushed the creature's limit, just as he hoped he would. He whipped out one of his swords and closed the distance before Vokar could pull his weapon from its scabbard.

"You need to calm down," said Atticus softly. "Now I don't give a rat's ass about you attacking that village. Do what you orcs usually do. But I am telling you that it is guarded by Etarian Knights and they will wipe out your clan unless you do what I suggest. Now, what is it going to be?"

"One day I kill you."

"One day you will try."

For a week Kaylen lay shivering on the ground covered only by a thin blanket. Each morning

Atticus came and talked to him and gave him a bowl of gruel with tough stringy meat and a cup of water. At first he refused the meal but as the week wore on he found his mind was losing focus so he took the offered food no matter how disgusting it was.

As he ate Atticus talked to him about a variety of things, both personal and about West End. Late at night he would weep inside the blanket fearing that he had sealed the fate of his home. What would Lars, Darius, and poor old Rurik think? Had he betrayed them?

After Atticus left, Kaylen managed to pull himself to the tree where he was shackled and prop his back against the trunk. He carefully watched the orc camp as they prepared for battle. The huge beasts were busy sharpening swords, axes, and spears. Other's worked on mismatched armor to make sure it was as strong as they could make it. If he had to guess Atticus thought there were nearly two hundred warriors who could fight. Enough to bring West End to its knees.

They were a strange species, Kaylen. They varied widely in appearance and resembled primitive humans with grey-green skin covered with coarse hair. Their posture was stooped with low jutting foreheads, and a snout instead of a nose. Their faces contained well-developed canine teeth and short pointed ears that resemble those of a wolf. The males stood around six foot tall on average he guessed while the females were somewhat shorter. Their clothing was somewhat to be desired with a mixture of blood red, rust, orange, and green.

A young orc stood nearby and stared at him with narrowed red eyes. Kaylen returned the look as the two took in each other.

"Come here," said Kaylen softly.

The orc cocked his head.

"Come here please."

It took some doing but the little creature eventually moved forward. They were there separated by three feet of frozen ground and just continued to stare. Poor little guy, thought Kaylen. If he lived twice his age he would face nothing but hardships among his tribe. But there was nothing he could do. He had to survive here and now.

"What is your name?" asked Kaylen.

"Talo," replied the youngling.

"Talo. My name is Kaylen Brightblade. How old are you Talo?"

"Ten winters."

Ten years old, thought Kaylen. If he were of a different race he would either be playing or doing simple chores for his parents. Instead he was with a tribe of brutes who preyed on others. In years to come he would be the same as those who raised him. Kaylen nodded to the adult orcs. "What are they doing Talo?"

"War," replied Talo. "War with humans. Village near. Orcs take village."

"Orcs take the village?" asked Kaylen. "But why? Why do your kin make war?"

"Orcs do war. Orcs like war. That is life of orc."

Too late, mused Kaylen. They had already corrupted his little mind. "When Talo? When do the orcs attack the village?"

Talo grew quiet. He looked around, his eyes watching to see if the adults caught him talking to the strange human. Finally he turned back to the knight. "Two days. Orcs attack village."

Two days. That gave Kaylen very little time to get out of here and warn West End. Even if he did he doubted everyone could escape the wrath of these beasts. But somehow he had to try.

"Talo!" bellowed a loud voice.

Vokar moved toward Kaylen, the assassin Atticus on his heels. Shit, thought the knight. He was doomed now. He had pushed the little creature for information but now he knew what was coming. Another beating from the orc chieftain or even worse the certain death that Atticus had promised him.

Just as Vokar neared and drew back his hand at Talo Kaylen spoke. "Stop!"

All eyes looked to Kaylen.

"Please don't Chief Vokar. He did no harm; he simply wanted to look at me, to see a human."

Vokar seemed confused for a moment and then let his arm drop. He growled to no one in particular but little Talo seemed to understand the threat. With fast feet the youngster ran away.

"Leave Vokar son alone," hissed the orc. "Vokar will kill if talk again. Vokar promise this."

The threat was given. The chieftain growled at both Kaylen and Atticus as he left the two humans together. When he was out of earshot the assassin leaned down.

"You are a fool," he whispered to Kaylen. "That stupid bastard will kill you if you talk to his son again."

"I didn't talk to him," lied Kaylen.

"Don't toy with me Kaylen. I've already had your life spared from him and his clan."

"Why? You were paid to kill me by someone and you've had more than a dozen chances to do it or have one of them brutes run a blade thru me. Why are you doing this?"

Atticus stared at him for a long moment. For the life of him Kaylen could not figure out what the killer was up to. He was doing nothing more than sparing him for some reason? But why?

"I have my reasons," said Atticus. "When I am ready you and I will have a meeting in which only one of us will survive. That I promise you."

"Yeah well right now I would place my money on this orc and his clan. They're preparing to take down West End and I don't really see me living my way out of this."

"Well if you play the game right you may get out of this little predicament and keep your hide intact."

Kaylen shook his head. "I don't know what to even think of you Atticus, do you know that?"

Atticus nodded. "I know. Neither do I."

The knight watched as the orc men gathered their weapons and begin the march into West End. For three days they had prepared and now they were ready to bring death upon West End. He tried to do a rough estimate of how long it would take Lord Markel and his men to arrive but shook his head in frustration. Blast it there was just no way to tell. He didn't even know if the village knew what was about to come their way.

"What about me?" asked Kaylen to Vokar as the orc was leaving.

The chieftain turned to him. "Vokar will kill when return," he said. "You will not have home when Vokar is done." He gave a sinister sort of laugh and walked down the incline from camp.

Kaylen didn't know how long he sat there but the orcs were out of sight by the time Atticus came from one of the hide tents. The assassin was dressed in black leather armor under his flowing cloak. His twin short swords were strapped across his back and he was just putting a dagger into his belt. He walked across the compound, the female orcs giving him a wide berth. As tough as they were, the knight figured the assassin's reputation preceded him wherever he went.

Atticus stopped near Kaylen, bent down, and then slid a key into the shackle wrapped around the knight's ankle. "Get up," he said through gritted teeth.

Kaylen didn't have to think long. This was it. He had enough of being tied down like a dog and this man's messing with his brain had reached its boiling point.

Kaylen jumped to his feet and smacked Atticus across the face with his fist. The assassin fell back and Kaylen saw his opportunity so he reached out and kicked him in the side as payback from his sore body. "That's for driving me crazy with your nonsense!"

Atticus rolled with the attack and came to his feet. His hand went for the dagger but stopped short. He wiped the blood from his lip and laughed. "Very well Lord Brightblade I will give that one to you." He tugged on his cloak and nodded toward the back of one of the tents. The two walked, Kaylen not even guessing what was up Atticus' sleeve. As they came to the rear of the tent he was surprised to see his horse fully saddled and ready to go. Next to it was another horse, this one as dark as the clothes his adversary wore.

"Let's go," he said.

With the conversation over the two saddled up and rode quickly out of the encampment. Atticus set a good pace toward West End with Kaylen riding behind him. When they were a few miles away the assassin pulled over to a pile of thick brush. He got off and ordered Kaylen to do the same. He pulled on the brush and motioned Kaylen towards it.

"There's your gear. You have five minutes and then I'm leaving without you."

Kaylen didn't say anything. He quickly donned his armor and strapped on his sword. Once again they went about business quickly and were soon on the road again toward town. As they traveled a million thoughts ran through his mind but Kaylen had no idea of which was true. He wasn't concerned for his wellbeing at this time. If Atticus wanted to kill him now he could have easily done so. He would deal with the assassin later after this was over but for now he was going to focus his attention on West End. At the orcs pace they could easily reach the town at nightfall. With their dark skin it and the early darkness of winter that would be the best time to attack or either right before dawn on the next day. With the town sleeping, he figured it would be closer to dawn.

Two questions plagued his mind. One, when would Markel arrive and two, would they have enough time to prepare the militia for battle. Either way, he felt as though the village was doomed.

Chapter Fourteen

Rurik made the sign of the cross and stood up. He gave a bow to the small alter and turned around. As he looked up he saw Lars and Darius standing in the doorway of the chapel.

"Orcs have been spotted," said Lars calmly. "They are about fifteen miles north of here slowly making their way south."

Rurik could only nod. "Aye. How many?"

"Couple hundred at least," said Darius. "Just north of where we took the others down."

"God have mercy on our souls. I don't think we can hold that many of them at bay on our own. Blast it! Where are Lord Markel and his men?"

The three men went immediately to the manor where they assembled the men that served as soldiers under Kaylen's command. Eleven men could not even have hopes of keeping the orcs out of the manor must lest the town below.

Lars turned to one of the soldiers. "Go get Edwin Delapost and Gabriel. Tell them to organize the militia and get here as fast as they can."

"That fat bastard and his little crony won't help," said a disgusted Darius. "This motley little crew is all we have."

The taller man shook his head. "They have no choice. They either fight or they die. Whatever decision they make its life or death." He turned to the soldier who stood by, unsure of which way to turn. "Go!"

As the man scampered away Lars turned back to Darius. "Suggestions?"

The men gathered about the hall table. A large map of the area was laid out and all eyes looked upon it. Rurik stood thinking for some time. "We'll have to open the gates Lars. The townspeople will have to come into Brightblade Manor. It's their only safe haven here."

"I agree Bishop. You should tend to your flock and get them here. Tell them to bring only what they can carry. Make sure they're bringing food with them."

"Nay Lars," replied the priest sternly. "I am going to stay here and fight."

"You will Bishop Ironhedge. I promise you that. Now please go and bring them into the safety of the manor."

"Fine," replied the dwarf. "But you better not attack without me."

"I won't."

Lars studied the map. The orcs would come across the plains and sweep down into the town from the north. That meant the north wall would be where they met the beasts. There was no way in or out from that direction thank God. The only way would be for them to flank the sides of the manor and come into the south gate.

"These are farmers Lars," said Darius.

Lars thought for a second before replying. "Aye, and farmers might not be the best with swords but they rely on bows to bring down game in the winter, do they not? We can place dozens on the north wall. While they pick off the bastards the rest of us can mount and protect the flanks."

"They'll be scared. You know that."

"We'll all be scared when this is through I tell you."

Heavy footsteps marched into the hall. Edwin Delapost strolled across the stones like he was the High Senator of Kesh himself. He looked at the men with a scowling gaze.

"What are you doing?" asked Edwin.

"Saving your fat pompous ass," hissed Darius.

Lars held up his hand. "Enough," he told his fellow warrior. He turned to Edwin. "We're going to be attacked by orcs. They'll be here in a few hours, dusk at the latest."

"How do you know?"

"Because I have been with them," said a voice entering the room.

All eyes turned quickly to the doorway.

Kaylen Brightblade walked calmly through the door and into the room. His head was dirty and bruised but he carried it high like any noble would. At his side was a man dressed in black. He was older and carried an essence of fright about him.

Lars and Darius went for their swords together once they realized who walked with their commander.

"Hold!" ordered Kaylen.

"But Lord, that is---," started Lars.

"Yes, it is. It is the man who tried to kill me in this very stronghold. But it is also the man who rescued me from those evil bastards that are coming this way."

All stood in silence. Kaylen stared at them, his look unwavering. "Am I not Kaylen Brightblade, Lord of this hall? Protector of West End?"

Lars nodded. "Aye Kaylen you are."

"Then do as I say. This man and I have business that one day we will decide. However this day we will work together against a common foe."

Atticus stood with a grin. The young man did have it in him to be a forceful leader. As he thought, Kaylen would one day make a worthy adversary and he would enjoy killing him. But other things had to be taken care of first.

Kaylen marched to the table. Lars quickly went over what they had to work with, which wasn't much. He told Kaylen what his plan was regarding the archers and the knight nodded in agreement. It was a good plan and he had left the right man in charge of the manor and town. It wasn't but a couple minutes later that the town of West End began coming into the manor. Kaylen sought out Riva who was starting to make room for their new guests.

"Kaylen!" she shouted when she saw him.

They ran to each other and hugged longer than friends should have. Kaylen kissed her fully on the lips, letting her know how he really felt. She returned the kiss, not pulling away, her hands rubbing the back of his matted hair.

"Oh Kaylen I heard the orcs are coming to attack!" she said excitedly.

"They are," Kaylen replied. "But I want you to stay out of sight. I want you to stay inside with the women and children."

"But I can fight!" she demanded.

"I know you can Riva. You don't have to prove that to me. But the women and children must be kept safe. You are the one to do that should the time come."

"Can you beat them?"

Kaylen thought for the briefest of moments. "Yes. I believe we can. I think the people will unite. Have we heard where Markel is?"

Riva shook her head. "We have no idea. He is supposed to be here by now."

"He should have been here already if it wasn't for the stupid politicians. Anyway, I have work to do."

With that Kaylen went to prepare for battle.

#####

"Charming place," said Atticus.

"I like to think so," replied Kaylen. "I would invite you to stay after this but I think that would not be a good idea."

"Probably not," replied the assassin.

They sat on their mounts with other cavalry before the north wall. Together there were twenty horsemen. On either side of them were two dozen men with a wide assortment of weapons including dull swords, spears, and axes that were normally used for everything but battle. The faces behind these makeshift weapons were nervous and their bodies twitched in a mixture of anticipation and fear. Above them on the ramparts of the manor stood a couple dozen older men and boys with bows who stood ready to defend their town.

"You know your outnumbered right?" asked Atticus. "At least two to one. Maybe even greater than that."

"I know," replied Kaylen with a blank expression.

"I could just kill you now and collect my money."

"You could try. My men would cut you down before you moved ten feet. The money wouldn't do you any good."

Atticus laughed. "So true. Ah, what the hell I'd rather kill orcs right now anyway. Someday I'll kill you."

This time Kaylen returned the laugh. "So it is settled. One day we will battle, but it won't be today."

The assassin shook his head. "No."

They turned from each other and waited.

Just as the sun was setting dark figures could be made out coming in from the plains. They were large creatures dressed in various patterns of armor and carrying large weapons that glittered in the last rays of light.

"Mother of God," someone swore.

"Quiet!" ordered Kaylen. He spurred his horse and turned around so that he faced the men dedicating themselves to defending their home. "Men of West End listen to me!"

All eyes bore upon the young knight. They saw their lord sitting on his horse, his young face tight and gaunt with the urging of battle. He looked older than he was and in such a short time they could tell that he had settled into his position as knight. This was where he would make his name, good or bad.

"Before us comes a horde of evil beings. They come with nothing but malice and hate for you and the way you live. They have no honor, they believe in pagan gods. They are the cursed beings that God has placed upon our world who worship the god of Hades. We are all that stands between them and our beloved town. I ask you now, men of West End, will you fight for your freedom? Will you fight for the lives you lead? If not you, then who? I will lead you but will you follow?"

No one knew who started it but weapons flew into the air and cheers erupted from the crowd. Satisfied that he had them, all Kaylen had to do now was hold his end of the bargain.

"Here they come," whispered Lars.

"Archers prepare," said Kaylen back to his second in command.

Lars reached to his saddle horn where multicolored flags were tied. He pulled a white flag and waved it. On the ramparts above Gabriel said something to the archers and bow strings were readied.

With Vokar in the lead, the orcs attacked. They came across the plain with fury and vengeance. Dozens upon dozens of gray/green figures armed with every weapon imaginable rushed toward the small manor. To reach it they had to move up the hill where the structure sat and that gave an advantage to the humans defending it. Orcs were not the smartest creatures on Aerola and it showed during the opening moments in battle.

Gabriel sighted down the arrow attached to his bow. His heart beat inside his chest like a hammer as the orcs began their assent on the hill. This wasn't like the normal backstreet brawl with a drunkard. He mentally cursed Kaylen Brightblade even though he knew his life depended on the young man to lead them through this nightmare.

"Fire!" yelled Gabriel.

He released the bowstring with a snap. The world seemed to go into slow motion for the young man. He watched the arrow make its flight thru the air and then as gravity took over the arrow made its fall toward the ground. The orc advancing never knew what hit him as the arrow fell at precisely the right angle and buried itself into a weak spot in the creature's armor. His massive arms flew wide and the orc fell dead. Gabriel swallowed hard and fought back the vile. He had just killed another living creature. It was then he realized that this wasn't a game any longer. This was real. He shook his head and then snapped back into the real world as his hand sought out another arrow.

"Damn kid's actually doing it," said Darius as orcs fell from the ramparts arrows. He turned to Kaylen. "Well Lord Brightblade? We are going to get into this?"

Kaylen looked to Atticus. "Thank you for bringing me back here. Someday maybe you'll tell me why you did this."

Atticus drew his twin short swords. "No. If you want to know you'll have to find out on your own." He gave Kaylen a bone chilling grin and urged his horse down the hill.

Kaylen shouted from the top of his lungs as he drew his sword from its scabbard. He kicked his horse and followed the assassin into the brewing battle below.

The cavalry launched itself toward the oncoming orcs, the men on foot following behind them but at a slower pace. The horsemen hit the orc line at full force. Horses jumped and their hooves bit into the orc flesh as though it was butter. Their riders slashed and stabbed with their weapons igniting screams of pain from the dark skinned beasts.

Dashing into the line Kaylen concentrated on his defense during the first few blows. He let his muscles settle into a rhythm of slashing blades. Kaylen spun left and right on his horse as he fought deep into the orc ranks. He swung at each turn, sometimes making a hit, sometimes a miss. His blade sank deep into an orc and blood shot out and covered his face. The young knight kept going leaving bodies in his wake. Screams and yelling from both sides didn't register in his mind. He ignored the blood and thought only of his own survival as one attacker went down another would be there. Kaylen fought for his life, for the lives of those he protected. There was no way he was going to let a single orc live to wreak havoc on the citizens of West End ever again.

Atticus had worked his way down the hill. He cared little for life, even less for orc life. With a holler he jumped from his steed and swung the twin swords in a wide arc. Two orcs went down with blood oozing from deadly wounds. Allies near him were wide eyed with fear more than they were from the orcs coming to meet them. The assassin was a blur of motion, turning and jumping at every possible angle while his weapons brought death on anyone near.

A group of orcs led by Vokar himself had worked their way up to the hill and were about to flank the east side of the manor. Behind them lay half dozen citizens posed in death. Darius saw this and charged the orc commander. He screamed as he slammed his body into the orc in hopes of knocking him off balance. The orc moved but only slightly. He swung a sword toward Darius' head but the young man ducked and stabbed toward the orc. The latter was more experienced though and side skipped the attack. Vokar bellowed a mighty roar. With one fluid motion he smacked his forehead toward Darius.

Darius' head exploded with pain as he staggered back. Suddenly his insides exploded in agony as the orc sent two massive punches into his stomach. He staggered again. His lungs ached for air and though it was now dark he felt his eyes go even blacker for a moment. As Darius fell to his knees his hand reached for a knife hidden in his boot. Just as his hand reached the hilt he felt the sudden rush of coldness in his chest. He gasped and felt the warm taste of blood in his mouth. Darkness came again. Darius somehow managed to look up into the face of Vokar.

"Puny human scum," hissed the orc commander. "You should have run away." He pulled out the sword and Darius shivered in agony. He slowly slipped to the ground and let the darkness overtake him.

Chapter Fifteen

Kaylen saw Darius fall under Vokar's blade. He charged up the hill in a blind rage taking every orc under his blade as he went. Behind him he could hear the hideous cackle of Atticus Bane as he dropped the beasts coming into his path. As they reached the top of the hill where the manor lay they could see the hulking shape of Vokar strolling along the eastern wall. Men cowered under his fearful growl and dropped their swords as they ran for cover.

Kaylen couldn't blame them. They were simple men and the sight of the large orc would send a trained soldier scampering to safety. Vokar was a chieftain because he showed no fear and was strong in every aspect of orc life. So when the knight and assassin caught him he simply stopped to face them. A wicked looking smile of bloody tusks glowed back at them.

"You are a traitor Atticus Bane," said Vokar.

Atticus shrugged. "Maybe young Brightblade here offered me more money? When he said he wanted to put a contract on you I turned him down though. I told him I'd do it for free."

"You are a fool. You should have died with your parents."

The smile faded from Atticus' face. For the first time since they met, Kaylen saw a different side of the assassin. It was almost human and for the briefest moment he thought he saw a tint of sadness. Sadness that soon faded into outright anger.

"Orc bastard," said Atticus.

The assassin lurched into frenzy. He swirled about the orc slashing out with his swords. The orc continued to smile and parried the blows with ease, seeming to ignore the attack that the assassin was trying to deliver.

Kaylen stood there watching. Dark orc blood mixed with his own from several wounds to his face and head. It dripped slowly down his face, mixing in with the grime of battle. There was something going on within Atticus. He could see it but wasn't for sure what it was. Regardless, the assassin kept up his attack on the large greenish beast.

The knight took a deep breath. The man who had tried to kill him needed help in defeating the beast and there was only one person who could help him do it. Somewhere deep inside him he found what energy he had left and leaped into battle.

It was said long after the battle that men and orcs both stopped to witness the event taking place before them. Two bloodied men were taking on one of the most powerful orcs in the land. With spear and sword Vokar deflected their blows and somehow managed to deliver some of his own. Back and forth, three warriors battled each other to the death.

Kaylen went in for an attack. He swung low then high. The orc was quick and managed to block both attacks. With the speed that the young knight had never seen before, the orc kicked out and Kaylen found himself falling back. As he was on the ground Atticus took his turn and brought both his swords down, aiming for Vokar's head. The orc noticed the oncoming attack so he turned and used his large sword to block the blow that only ended in a shower of sparks. He shoved with all his might and the assassin went back as well.

Now that both humans were off balance Vokar took his turn at going in on the offensive. He felt the young knight to be the lesser enemy and swung both his weapons in Kaylen's direction. Kaylen sensed this and blocked the spear by knocking it away. However the point of the orc's sword caught him in the thigh and he went down. Kaylen gritted his teeth with pain.

Atticus saw the orc going for Kaylen. He took the chance and rushed in. Vokar's back was exposed so the assassin swung his swords in opposite directions across the dark skin of his enemy. Two lines of blood appeared but the orc didn't seem to notice. Atticus went in to do a back thrust but the orc was used to battle and knew how to handle himself. He spun on his heel and struck the assassin across the face with a meaty hand. Atticus felt his lip split and he cursed as blood gushed from his mouth.

"You stupid fucking piece of shit," shouted Atticus. "I curse you and your kind until hell freezes over!"

The orc howled. He was getting furious with the two humans and it was time to end this once and for all.

Both Atticus and Kaylen knew this was their chance. The orc had let his emotions control him and they quickly regained their own composure as they moved in. If they were going to take him it had to be now.

Slashes and stabs rocked at the orc's body. The latter now howled but not in anger so much as in pain. He thrust out his chest to try and intimidate them with his large body and powerful strength. He swung his sword at both men. Now back to back, the two men moved like cats and squeezed their way past the deadly blade. As they did so both shot out with their own weapons and pierced the chest of the orc.

Vokar roared in misery through the night air sending shivers to anyone who heard it. Kaylen and Atticus removed their blades at the same time and each swung on opposite sides of the orc's side. Both blades snapped through the cheap metal and pierced the meaty flesh underneath. Blood spurted and gushed. Black blood, the blood of death.

Vokar stumbled as blood oozed from countless wounds. He let out a pitiful squeal as he fell to his death. The two humans stood in pants eyeing the fallen chieftain. Slowly they looked into each other's eyes. Would they put an end to it now? Would they now fight each other and be done with their own personal business? No. Death had enough victims tonight. He could wait another day.

Kaylen stood looking out over the rampart walls at West End. It was a winter day but the sun was out and despite the chill in the air, people were out enjoying each other's company. From time to time someone would notice him and wave in his direction. From this distance Kaylen couldn't tell who it was but would wave back, glad that they accepted his new position.

He turned to see Lars walking in his direction. Like Kaylen, he bore the scars of recent battle. He winced as he approached.

"You okay?" laughed Kaylen.

"I'll live," replied Lars with a smile. "I have news. Lord Markel is about two miles out. He'll be here within the hour with his troop."

"Perfect timing," snorted Kaylen in sarcasm. "I guess I better prepare for his arrival. Tell Riva we're having guests for lunch."

"Aye, milord."

Kaylen walked down a flight of steps to the courtyard where his favorite figure in black sat atop his horse. The assassin looked down at him with tired eyes and a swollen lip.

"Leaving?" asked Kaylen.

"Ugh yes," replied Atticus. "I hear Lord Markel and a hundred of his finest are near. I don't really need that sort of attention right now. Don't really think these old bones can handle it."

"What? The great Atticus Bane can't handle a troop of Etarian soldiers?"

Atticus' face grew stern. "We will meet again Lord Brightblade, of that I am sure. When I ride out these gates we will be enemies again. This you know. But I do have something to give you."

Kaylen's eyebrows arched. Was he going to try and kill him now? Atticus reached into the folds of his cloak and withdrew something. He tossed it to Kaylen who caught it in his hands with a jingle. The young knight trembled. Was this what he thought it was?

"W-who hired you Atticus?" he stuttered.

The assassin shook his head. "Can't tell you. You know that. But can I give you some advice? Stay away from Brulan. Life will be much better for you out here on the edge of the wilderness."

Kaylen nodded. "Where will you go?"

Atticus shook his head. "I don't know. I think somewhere out of your country. Goodbye Lord Kaylen Brightblade." He spurred his horse and let the knight stand there in thought. At the gate the assassin spun his horse on its hooves.

"Oh by the way Lord Brightblade," he said. "Tell Lady Isabella hello from me."

Kaylen's knees went weak. He looked down at the pouch of coins with a sick feeling in his stomach. He raised his head but Atticus Bane was nowhere to be seen. So he stood there, lost in thought. There were a lot of things to discuss, a lot of things to think about. But for right now his place was here, at the manor. This was his home. He was Lord Kaylen Brightblade, the Bastard Knight of Kesh. One day he would find Atticus Bane again and they would have a long hard talk. But for now he decided to wait. It would take time to heal and then maybe he would make a visit to Brulan. After all, he hadn't seen his dear family in quite some time. He was long overdue for a visit.

Kaylen whistled to himself and with that, he walked toward the hall to await his guests.

THE END